Winter Wishes & Elven Kisses

Evershift Haven, Volume 3

Aurelia Skye and Kit Tunstall

Published by Amourisa Press, 2024.

Blurb

I, Evony Johnson, am a Chicago accountant who lives for spreadsheets and numbers—until my best friend's magical town decides I need a frosty holiday romance with their resident winter elf.

WHEN MY BEST FRIEND Candice invited me to spend Christmas in Evershift Haven, I expected a quaint small town with over-the-top decorations. Instead, I've stumbled into a magical wonderland, where pumpkins become carriages, trees whisper gossip, and the most gorgeous elf I've ever seen keeps giving me smoldering looks. Frost Evergreen runs the town's magical gift shop, and he claims he's been dreaming about me for centuries. Talk about pressure on a first date—but there's something about his silver hair, color-changing eyes, and the way snowflakes dance when he smiles that makes me warmer than the magical concoctions at the town's coffee shop.

Between saving the town's Christmas magic and discovering my own hidden fae heritage, I'm falling hard for this winter wonderland—and its enchanting shopkeeper. When the holiday season ends, will I choose to return to my life in Chicago? Or will I embrace the magic that Evershift Haven, and Frost, are offering?

Welcome back to Evershift Haven, where magic sparkles in every season, holiday celebrations always include a dash of chaos, and love stories are sprinkled with literal stardust. This third book in the series wraps you in all the cozy warmth of hot cocoa and holiday magic, with enough heat to melt the winter frost.

Chapter 1

I GRIP THE STEERING wheel of my red convertible as I approach the shimmering barrier surrounding Evershift Haven. Candice practically bounces in the passenger seat, her excitement obvious. She's been like this ever since she met me a few minutes ago, on the outskirts of this mysterious town to where she and her sister, Suzette, have moved.

"Come on, Evony. Just drive through. It's perfectly safe, I promise."

I roll my eyes. "Right. Because driving through an invisible wall is totally normal." Nothing about this visit is normal, and I'm worried for my friends. Candi though Suz might be mixed up in a cult when she came to visit, and then she invited me. I'm wary, to say the least.

"It's not invisible," says Candice. "Look at how it sparkles."

I squint, and sure enough, there's a faint shimmer in the air, like heat rising from hot pavement. "This is insane," I mutter, but I press the gas pedal anyway. The barrier flashes as we pass through, and a tingling sensation washes over my skin. I blink rapidly, disoriented.

"See? Told you it was fine." Candice grins.

I shake my head, trying to clear the lingering dizziness. "Okay, so we made it through your magic forcefield. Now what?"

"Now," says Candice, practically vibrating with excitement, "We drive to my new place. You won't believe it, Ev. It's amazing. We moved Ronan's cabin and added a...special addition.

I arch a brow, wondering what's so special about it Oh, right, magic. My friend is either crazy or in a cult.

While driving, I notice the landscape changing. The trees seem...greener somehow, their leaves shimmering with an otherworldly light. There's snow in the air and on the ground, as one would expect in Montana at Christmastime, but there are also flowers blooming in impossible colors. I swear I see one turn to follow our car as we pass.

"Candice," I say slowly, "What's going on with the plants?"

She laughs. "Oh, that's just the enchanted flora. Wait till you see the talking sunflowers. Or the gourds. I could spend hours talking to them."

I grip the steering wheel tighter. "The what-now?"

Before she can answer, we round a bend, and I slam on the brakes. A massive, glittering unicorn stands in the middle of the road, munching on what appears to be a bush made of cotton candy. "What the actual f—"

"Language," says Candice, looking dismayed. "Unicorns are very sensitive to swearing."

The unicorn turns its head, fixing us with an imperious stare. It snorts, tossing its mane, before trotting off into the woods.

I turn to Candice, my mouth hanging open. She just grins and points ahead. "Keep driving. We're almost there."

Numbly, I put the car back in gear and continue down the winding road. My mind races, trying to make sense of what I'm seeing. Fairies flit around the windshield. A gnome waves cheerfully from his front yard. A group of what can only be described as walking, talking mushrooms crosses the street in front of us.

"Candice," I say, my voice strained, "I think I'm having a mental breakdown."

She pats my arm. "Nope. You're just experiencing magic for the first time. Isn't it wonderful?"

I don't answer, too focused on not crashing as we navigate through this impossible landscape. Finally, we pull up to a clearing, containing a cabin attached to a...giant onion?

"We're here." Candice leaps out of the car before I've fully stopped.

I park and slowly get out, staring at the enormous vegetable before me. It's easily the size of a small house, its papery skin a soft golden color. A door and windows have been carved into its side, and smoke curls from a chimney poking out of the top.

"You live...in an onion?" I ask, incredulous.

"Grizelda designed it for us to expand the cabin's size when we moved to Ronan's land so I could start my farm. Oh, so much to tell you." Candice beams. "Isn't it perfect? Come on, I'll give you the tour."

She grabs my hand, pulling me toward the onion-house. I dig in my heels, resisting.

"Candice, wait. What is all this? What's going on?"

She turns, her expression softening. "Oh, Ev. I know it's a lot to take in. I thought Suzette was in a cult when she told me about it, remember?" She giggles.

"I'm not convinced you both haven't fallen victim to a cult," I say bluntly.

She shakes her head, not looking offended. "Evershift Haven is a magical town, hidden from the rest of the world. Remember all those stories we used to read as kids? The ones about fairies and unicorns and magic? They're all real."

I shake my head. "That's impossible. Magic isn't real. This has to be some kind of... I don't know, mass hallucination or elaborate prank or—"

"Or magic," she says gently. "I know it's hard to believe, but you've seen it with your own eyes. The barrier, the plants, the unicorn—"

"That could all be special effects or holograms or—"

Candice sighs, then snaps her fingers. Instantly, her hair begins to change color, cycling through a rainbow of hues before settling back to its natural blonde.

I stumble backward. "How did you do that?"

She grins. "Magic. I've been practicing. Cool, right?"

I stare at her, my mind reeling. Everything I thought I knew about the world is crumbling around me. "This can't be happening," I whisper.

She takes my hands in hers. "I know it's overwhelming, but think about it, Ev. You've been searching for your 'thing' for so long. Maybe this is it. Maybe magic is what you've been missing all along."

I look around the clearing, taking in the impossible sights. The flowers popping out of the snow, the shimmering air, and the giant onion house. Part of me wants to run screaming back to the barrier, to the safe, logical world I've always known.

But another part, a part I've kept buried for years, feels a spark of excitement. Of wonder. Of possibility. "Okay," I say slowly. "Let's say, hypothetically, that I believe you. That all of this is real. What does that mean for me?"

She smiles. "It means you get to explore a whole new world. There's so much to see and learn here, and who knows? Maybe you'll discover your own magical talents."

I raise an eyebrow. "You think I might be magical?"

She shrugs. "Only one way to find out. So, what do you say? Want to give Evershift Haven a chance?"

I inhale sharply before exhaling, looking from Candice to the onion house to the magical forest beyond. Everything in me screams that this is crazy, impossible, and dangerous, but there's a flicker of excitement. "All right," I say, squaring my shoulders. "Show me this magical world of yours."

Candice squeals, pulling me into a tight hug. "You won't regret this, Ev. Come on, let's start with a tour of my onion."

As she leads me toward the improbable vegetable dwelling, I wonder what other impossibilities await me in Evershift Haven. For better or worse, it seems my life is about to change dramatically.

And honestly? I'm kind of looking forward to it.

I approach the giant onion house, my eyes wide with disbelief. The golden, papery skin shimmers in the sunlight, and I can't shake the feeling that I've stumbled into some bizarre fairytale.

"Welcome to our humble abode," Candice says, gesturing grandly at the oversized vegetable. "Grizelda really outdid herself with this one."

"Grizelda," I repeat, trying to keep my voice steady. "The town witch, who apparently grows houses from produce?" I think that's what she told me in her email.

"She also keeps the barrier between us and the human world standing...most of the time." Candice laughs. "She's amazing, isn't she? Come on, let's go inside."

Nearing the entrance, a faint, familiar scent wafts through the air. I wrinkle my nose. "Is that..."

"Onion?" Candice finishes. "Yep, but don't worry. It's not overwhelming. Just a little reminder of our home's origins."

She pushes open the door, and I step inside, bracing myself for... I don't know what. The interior is surprisingly normal at first glance—a cozy living room with comfortable-looking furniture and warm, earthy tones, but as I look closer, I notice the subtle details that betray the house's unusual nature.

The walls curve gently, following the natural shape of the onion. Light filters through the papery skin, creating a golden glow throughout the space. In one corner, a small fountain bubbles, the water a pale purple color.

"That's onion juice," she says, noticing my stare. "It's great for purifying the air and keeping away pests. Plus, it makes the whole place smell amazing."

I raise an eyebrow. "Amazing" isn't the word I'd use to describe the scent of onions, but I have to admit, it's not unpleasant. It's more like a hint of savory warmth in the air.

She leads me through the living room and into the kitchen. Here, the onion theme is more pronounced. The countertops are a pale, creamy color with subtle striations that mimic onion layers. The light fixtures are shaped like onion blossoms, casting a warm, diffused light.

"Check this out," says Candice, opening a cabinet. Inside, rows of jars filled with various-colored liquids line the shelves. "Onion preserves. They're not just for eating—some have magical properties. This red one here? Great for soothing burns, and the green? Helps plants grow faster."

I nod, pretending this is all perfectly normal. "Of course. Magical onion juice. Why not?"

Candice grins, either missing or ignoring my sarcasm. "I know, right? It's amazing what you can do with a little magic and a lot of onions."

We continue the tour, moving into a small study. Bookshelves line the walls, filled with tomes on subjects I never knew existed. "A Beginner's Guide to Magical Farming," "101 Uses for Enchanted Produce," and "The Secret Language of Vegetables" are just a few of the titles I spot.

"This is where I do most of my research. Magical farming is fascinating, but there's so much to learn. I'm lucky my mentor, Puckley, is as eager to share her knowledge as I am to acquire it."

I pick up a book titled "Communicating with Your Crops: A Comprehensive Guide." "You actually talk to your plants?"

Candice nods enthusiastically. "Oh, yes. They have so much to say once you learn how to listen. The tomatoes are terrible gossips, and the carrots tell the best jokes."

I set down the book carefully, wondering if I've finally lost my mind. "Right. Talking vegetables. Got it."

We move on to the bedroom, which is surprisingly normal compared to the rest of the house. A large, comfortable-looking bed dominates the space, with soft, cream-colored linens. The only hint of the room's unusual location is the curved ceiling and the faint, oniony scent that permeates the air.

"And here's my favorite part," says Candice, leading me to a spiral staircase in the corner of the room. We climb up, emerging into a small, circular space at the very top of the onion.

The room is entirely enclosed in the thin, translucent skin of the onion. Sunlight filters through, bathing everything in a warm, golden glow. A comfortable-looking chair sits in the center, surrounded by potted plants of all varieties.

"This is my meditation space. It's perfect for connecting with nature and honing my magical abilities."

I walk to the edge of the room, placing my hand against the onion skin. It's surprisingly sturdy, with a slightly waxy texture. "This is incredible. I still can't believe it's real, but it's incredible."

Candice beams. "I'm so glad you like it. Want to see how it connects to Ronan's cabin?"

We descend the stairs and exit the onion house through a different door than we entered. This one leads directly into a more traditional log cabin. The transition is jarring—from the whimsical, vegetable-inspired decor to rugged, masculine furnishings.

"This is Ronan's place. We moved the whole cabin here when we decided to combine our living spaces."

I look around, taking in the sturdy wooden furniture, the pelts on the walls, and the enormous fireplace. "You moved an entire cabin? How is that even possible?"

She shrugs. "Magic, of course. Grizelda and some of the other witches helped. It was quite a spectacle—the whole cabin floating through the air like a giant Monopoly piece."

I shake my head, trying to picture it. "And Ronan was okay with attaching a giant onion to his home?"

"Oh, he loves it." She grins. "He says it adds character. Plus, the onion juice really helps with the wet dog smell when he comes back from a run."

I blink. "Wet dog smell?"

Candice's eyes widen. "Oh, right. I forgot to mention Ronan's a lycan. You know, a werewolf, kind of, except he doesn't shift. More like a wolfman, I guess? He's a perfect gentleman though. Most of the time, anyway." She waggles her eyebrows suggestively and flushes, transmitting when she appreciates him not being a gentleman.

I sink into the nearest chair, my head spinning. Magic, talking vegetables, onion houses, and now werewolves...er, wolfmen? It's too much to process.

Candice kneels beside me, her expression concerned. "I know it's a lot to take in, but isn't it exciting? A whole new world of possibilities."

I look at the woman who's been my friend for years. She seems so at home here, so happy. Part of me wants to run screaming from this insanity, but another part...is curious. Excited, even.

"Okay," I say slowly. "I'm not saying I believe all of this yet, but I'm willing to keep an open mind. Tell me more about this magical farming you're getting into."

Her smile widens. "Let me show you the plans for my enchanted vegetable garden. Did you know that with the right spells, you can grow watermelons that never run out of fruit? Or tomatoes that change flavor based on your mood?"

As she launches into an enthusiastic explanation of magical agriculture, I'm fascinated despite my skepticism. Maybe there's more to this world than I ever imagined. Perhaps, in this strange town of Evershift Haven, I might discover a part of myself I never knew existed.

THE NEXT MORNING, AFTER meeting Ronan and having dinner with Suzette and Throk as well, who joined us in the onion house, I'm no longer able to disbelieve in magic. How can I after meeting a lycan and an orc?

Still somewhat in a daze, I step out of Candice's onion house, blinking in the bright winter sunlight. Snowflakes dance in the air, each one a perfect, glittering crystal. The sight is breathtaking, but something's off about them.

"Are these snowflakes...magical?" I ask, eyeing them suspiciously.

Candice laughs, her breath forming little puffs in the cold air. "Of course. They're Frost's special creation. He makes them extra sparkly for the holidays."

I shake my head, still not used to casual mentions of magic. "Right. Of course, he does." I don't ask who Frost is, positive that I'll meet him soon enough.

"Come on," says Candice, linking her arm through mine. "We've got some serious Christmas shopping to do."

As we walk down the winding path toward town, I marvel at the winter wonderland around us. Every tree is perfectly frosted, icicles hanging from branches like crystal chandeliers, and the temperature is still perfectly pleasant in just a sweater and scarf. It's beautiful, but almost too perfect.

"So, where are we going first?" I ask, trying to focus on the task at hand rather than the impossibility of our surroundings.

Candice grins. "'Frost's Festive Finds.' It's the best place for Christmas shopping in Evershift Haven."

We walk a bit more, and I experience the various sights and sounds of the town as we stroll. It's wonderful but overwhelming.

Suddenly, we round a corner, and I stop in my tracks. Before us stands a massive structure that looks like it's been carved entirely from ice. Intricate frost patterns swirl across its surface, and warm light spills from windows that shouldn't be possible in a building made of frozen water.

"That's a store?" I ask, incredulous.

Candice nods enthusiastically. "Isn't it amazing? Frost redesigns it every year, so each Christmas, it looks different. Let's go inside."

She pulls me toward the entrance, and I brace myself for a blast of cold air. To my surprise, it's comfortably warm inside. The interior is a Christmas lover's dream—twinkling lights, garlands of evergreen, and displays of ornaments and gifts as far as the eye can see.

"Wow," I say, taking it all in.

"I know, right?" Candice beams. "Okay, let's split up. I need to find something for Suzette."

Before I can protest, she disappears into the crowd, leaving me alone in this magical emporium. I wander through the aisles, marveling at the items on display. A snow globe that creates a miniature blizzard when shaken. A string of lights that change color based on the mood in the room. A wreath that sings carols in perfect harmony.

I'm so engrossed in examining a set of ornaments that seem to contain entire galaxies that I don't notice someone approaching until a smooth, cool voice speaks right next to my ear.

"Fascinating, aren't they? Each one contains a pocket dimension—an entire universe in the palm of your hand."

I jump, nearly dropping the delicate orb. A tall, impossibly handsome man stands beside me, his skin so pale it almost glows. Long, silver-white hair is pulled back in an intricate braid, and his eyes... I blink, certain I must be seeing things. Starting out vibrant green, they abruptly shift color, from icy blue to deep purple to shimmering silver.

"I... What?" I stammer, struggling to process both his words and his appearance.

He smiles, and it's like watching frost spread across a windowpane—beautiful, but somehow cold. "You must be new here. Evony, correct? Candice's friend?"

I nod, not trusting myself to speak.

"Frost Evergreen," he says, extending a hand. "Welcome to my humble establishment."

I shake his hand, surprised by how warm it is despite his wintry appearance. "Nice to meet you. This place is incredible."

His smile widens, but it doesn't quite reach his ever-changing eyes. "Thank you. I do pride myself on creating the ultimate holiday shopping experience." He pauses, sweeping his gaze over me in a way that makes me feel like I'm being assessed. "Though I must say, I'm not sure we need yet another human tilting the magical balance around here."

I bristle at his words, opening my mouth to retort, but before I can speak, he winks at me. The gesture is so unexpected, so at odds with his aloof demeanor, that I'm left speechless.

"Of course," he continues smoothly, "Who am I to argue with the will of the ley lines? If they've drawn you here, there must be a reason."

I find my voice at last. "Look, I don't know anything about ley lines or magical balance. I'm just here to do some Christmas shopping with my friend, who invited me to this crazy town."

He chuckles, and the sound is like icicles tinkling in the wind. "Of course, you are. Well, don't let me keep you. Do let me know if you need any assistance finding the perfect gift. I have an eye for these things, you know."

With that, he glides away, leaving me staring after him in confusion. What a strange, infuriating man. Elf. Whatever he is.

I shake my head, trying to clear it, and return my attention to the shelves around me. I still need to find gifts for my family back in the "real world," as Candice calls it. How am I supposed to explain any of these magical items to them?

As I browse, I try and fail not to notice Frost moving through the store. He straightens displays that are already perfect, advises customers with an air of superiority, and generally acts like he's the king of Christmas itself. It's irritating, but I also can't seem to take my gaze off him.

There's something magnetic about him, a charisma that draws the eye despite his cold demeanor. He helps an elderly woman select a scarf that changes pattern to match her outfit, and his movements are graceful and precise. When he smiles at her, it's warmer than the ones he gave me, and I feel an inexplicable pang of...something. Envy? Ridiculous.

I force myself to focus on my shopping, selecting a few "normal" items that won't raise suspicion back home. A cozy sweater for Mom, a leather-bound journal for Dad, and some artisanal chocolates for my sister. I find a collection of stationary for my grandmother. As I make my way to the counter, I'm face-to-face with Frost once again.

"Find everything you were looking for?" he asks, his tone polite but distant.

"Yes, thank you," I say, trying to match his coolness.

He begins ringing up my purchases, moving his long fingers with inhuman speed and grace. "No magical items?" he asks, raising an eyebrow. "How...quaint."

I bristle at his condescending tone. "My family doesn't know about all this," I gesture vaguely around us, "And I'd like to keep it that way."

He pauses, fixing me with those mesmerizing, color-shifting eyes. "Ah, yes. The great secret. Tell me, Evony, how long do you think you'll be able to keep this world hidden from them? Magic has a way of seeping through the cracks."

His words make me shiver. "What do you mean?"

He smiles enigmatically. "Oh, nothing to worry about, I'm sure. That'll be forty-seven fifty."

I hand over the money with a frown. As he gives me my change, our fingers brush, and I swear I feel a spark of...something. Magic? Static electricity? My imagination running wild?

"Thank you for your patronage," he says, his tone formal once again. "Do come again. Who knows? Perhaps next time you'll be ready for something a bit more enchanting."

As I turn to leave, I catch sight of my reflection in a nearby mirror. For just a moment, I could swear I see a faint shimmer around me, like the air itself is sparkling. I blink, and it's gone.

LATER THAT EVENING, accompanying Candice and Ronan, I step into the town square, marveling at the transformation unfolding. Just earlier today, Evershift Haven was awash in the warm hues of autumn. Now, it's morphing into a winter wonderland right before my gaze.

Snowflakes materialize in the air, each one a perfect, unique crystal. They dance on an unfelt breeze, swirling in intricate patterns before settling on the ground. The cobblestones, previously dry and warm, now sparkle with a light dusting of snow that doesn't melt.

"How is this possible?" I whisper, watching as bare tree branches suddenly sprout evergreen needles.

Candice grins beside me. "It's the seasonal shift. Evershift Haven has a mind and magic of its own and seems to know innately when it's time to change—though it can also change for random reasons, like a welcoming ceremony, or a baby shower. Grizelda's just officiating it."

As if on cue, Grizelda appears in the center of the square. In a way, she looks exactly like I'd expect a witch to look, with silver-streaked purple hair and seafoam green skin, but she's pretty. Not a wart in sight. Her wild mane of hair seems to move of its own accord, and her vibrant purple eyes glow with an inner light. She raises her arms, and the air around her shimmers.

"Hello, citizens of Evershift Haven." Her voice rings out, magically amplified. "It's time to welcome the winter season and especially, Christmas."

With a dramatic flourish of her hands, a wave of magic ripples outward from the center of the town, near her but clearly not originating *from* her. I gasp as it passes through me, leaving a tingling sensation in its wake. The transformation accelerates.

Pumpkins on doorsteps morph into perfectly round snowmen, complete with coal eyes and carrot noses. Piles of gourds decoratively arranged transform into ornate ice sculptures. Autumn leaves still clinging to trees change into delicate icicles that chime softly in the breeze.

Storefronts shift before my eyes. "The Enchanted Espresso's" exterior turns a crisp white, with peppermint-striped awnings appearing over the windows. "Frost's Festive Finds," already Christmas-themed, grows even more elaborate. The ice structure seems to expand, sprouting delicate spires and arches.

"This is incredible," I say, turning in a slow circle to take it all in.

Candice nods enthusiastically. "Wait until you see the best part."

As if on cue, the massive oak tree in the center of the square—the Heart of Haven, Ronan tells me as an aside—begins to change. Its bare branches fill out with lush evergreen needles. Twinkling lights appear, wrapping around the trunk and spiraling up into the branches. Ornaments in every color imaginable materialize, hanging from the boughs.

"Citizens," says Grizelda, "I'm pleased to report our protective barrier remains strong and stable. We can look forward to another peaceful holiday season in Evershift Haven."

The crowd cheers, but I notice something off about Grizelda. Her skin, previously a seafoam green, suddenly looks pale and washed out. She sways slightly, and Atlas, her towering troll husband, moves to support her.

"Candice," I whisper, nudging my friend. "Is Grizelda okay? She doesn't look well."

Candice's eyes widen. "Oh, I forgot you didn't know. Grizelda's pregnant."

I blink in surprise. "Pregnant? But she looks...well, older."

Candice giggles. "Grizelda's over a hundred years old, but that's not too old for a witch. This pregnancy has been causing some magical mayhem though. Last week, all the books in the library started reading themselves out loud. The week before that, every mirror in town only showed people's auras instead of their reflections."

I shake my head, still struggling to process the idea of magical pregnancy side effects. My attention is drawn back to the Heart of Haven. The massive tree seems to pulse with an inner light, but something about it seems off. The glow flickers erratically, like a faulty light bulb.

"Candice, what's happening with the tree? Is it supposed to do that?"

Before Candice can answer, a cool voice speaks from directly behind me. "No, it most certainly isn't."

I whirl around to find Frost standing there, his silver-white hair gleaming in the magical light. His eyes, currently a stormy gray, are fixed on the Heart of Haven with a look of concern.

"What do you mean?" I ask, my heart racing at his sudden appearance. "What's wrong with it?"

He shifts his gaze to me, and I suppress a shiver. "The Heart of Haven is more than just a tree, Evony. It's the magical core of our town, and the anchor point for the protective barrier that keeps us hidden from the human world."

I glance back at the flickering tree. "And it's not supposed to flicker like that?"

"No. The Heart should pulse with a steady, constant light. This erratic behavior is...concerning."

Candice frowns. "But Grizelda just said the barrier was stable."

His expression darkens. "Grizelda has been...distracted lately. Her pregnancy is affecting her magic in ways we didn't anticipate. I fear she might be overlooking signs of trouble."

A chill runs through me that has nothing to do with the magical winter around us. "What kind of trouble?"

He opens his mouth to respond, but before he can, a loud crack echoes through the square. We all turn to see a large branch from the Heart of Haven crash to the ground, scattering ornaments and sending a shower of sparks into the air.

Gasps and murmurs ripple through the crowd. Grizelda stumbles forward, her face ashen. "It's fine," she calls out, her voice shaky. "Just a bit of magical overflow. Nothing to worry about."

As I look from Grizelda's pale face to Frost's concerned frown to the flickering, damaged Heart of Haven, I think there's plenty to worry about indeed.

Chapter 2

I'VE BEEN IN EVERSHIFT Haven for a whole week now, and I'm still adjusting. It's Christmas Eve, and the bell above "The Enchanted Espresso's" door chimes a festive tune as I step inside with Suzette and Candice. Holiday garlands wrap the exposed wooden beams, and the scent of peppermint and chocolate fills the air.

"Welcome." Bella waves from behind the counter, her curly hair sparkling with what appears to be actual snowflakes. "You're just in time to try our December special—the Reindeer's Delight."

"What's in it?" I eye the drink she's preparing, which sparkles and shifts colors like the northern lights. Suzette mentioned bunny ears before we stopped in, so I'm wary.

"Hot chocolate infused with winter magic, topped with whipped cream that tastes like fresh snow, and a sprinkle of enchanted cinnamon." Bella's eyes twinkle. "It used to give people temporary elf ears, until Frost complained it was 'culturally insensitive.' Now, it just gives you adorable reindeer antlers for an hour."

"Antlers?" I raise an eyebrow. "You're joking."

"Not at all." Candice bounces on her toes. "Watch this." She takes a sip of her drink, and small, velvet-covered antlers sprout from her blonde hair almost immediately. "See?"

"This town gets weirder by the day," I say but accept the mug Bella hands me. The drink tastes like childhood winter memories and cozy fireside evenings. A warm tingling spreads across my scalp. I touch my head, finding small antlers growing. "This is ridiculous." I'm grinning as I say it though.

"Speaking of winter magic," Bella leans across the counter, "We need everyone's help decorating the town square today. Evershift Haven's magic handles most of it, but there are always gaps to fill in."

"Gaps?" asks Suzette.

"The town's magic creates most decorations, but sometimes, it misses spots. That's where we come in—hanging extra lights, adding ornaments, and making sure every corner sparkles."

"The whole town helps?" I ask.

"Everyone pairs up and takes a section." Bella grins. "In fact, we should head over now. The assignments are about to start."

The town square buzzes with activity when we arrive. Frost stands in the center, directing people with precise gestures. His silver hair catches the winter sunlight, and his pointed ears peek through the intricate braid.

"Ah, perfect timing." He spots our group. "Evony, you'll work with me on the central display."

I open my mouth to protest, but he's already walking away, expecting me to follow.

"These garlands need precise placement," he says, not looking back. "The angles must be exact for proper magical flow."

"Right." I roll my eyes. "Heaven forbid we just hang them where they look nice."

He turns, currently ice-blue eyes narrowing. "This isn't about aesthetics. The decorations channel magical energy. A human wouldn't understand."

"Try me." I cross my arms. "I'm an accountant. I understand precise measurements and calculations better than most."

"Numbers on paper are different from centuries of magical tradition."

"Maybe. Or maybe you're just stuck in your ways and afraid to try something new."

A few snowflakes swirl around him as his eyes flash, turning almost black. "I've been doing this for three hundred years."

"And how many of those years did you actually try something different?"

His nostrils flare, and he opens his mouth to retort when a loud crack echoes through the square. We both turn to see a string of lights plummet from the sky, narrowly missing a group of startled elves.

"What was that?" I ask, my heart still racing.

Frost's expression shifts from anger to concern. "The Heart of Haven. Something's wrong."

As if on cue, more decorations begin to fall. Garlands slither across the ground like tinsel snakes, and ornaments bounce erratically, shattering against cobblestones.

"Look out," I shout, pulling Frost aside as a massive wreath tumbles past us.

He grabs my arm, steadying me. Our gazes lock, and for a second, there's a definite...sizzle between us. then he blinks and drops his hand. "We need to get to the center of town. Now."

We weave through the chaos, dodging rogue decorations and panicked townsfolk. The closer we get to the town's center, the more pronounced the magical glitches become. Storefronts flicker like faulty neon signs, and the very air seems to shimmer and warp.

An enormous oak tree stands in the heart of the square, its branches reaching toward the sky. Instead of the vibrant, glowing entity I saw earlier, the tree now pulses with a sickly, dim light.

"The Heart of Haven," Frost whispers, his voice filled with awe and fear. "It's failing."

I stare at the tree, mesmerized by its fading glow. "What does that mean?"

Frost's face is grim. "It means we're in serious trouble. The Heart of Haven is the source of our town's magic, carefully tended by a caretaker—Grizelda for now, and a different witch when she retires. If it fails completely..." He trails off, clearly alarmed.

My mouth is dry all of a sudden. "What happens if it fails?"

He frowns. "If the Heart fails, the barrier protecting Evershift Haven will collapse, and without that barrier, Santa's portal won't open."

I blink, trying to process this information. "Santa's portal? You mean, Santa Claus is real too?"

A ghost of a smile flickers across Frost's face. "Of course, he's real, though he's fae—Elven, to be exact—not human. Evershift Haven is a key stop on his route. Our magic helps power his sleigh for the long journey."

Another crack splits the air, and the tree's glow further dims. Frost winces as if in physical pain.

"So, what happens if Santa can't get here?" I ask, dreading the answer.

His tone is full of anguish. "Then Evershift Haven loses its Christmas magic, and without that..." He gestures around us. "All of this becomes harder to maintain. Our home, our way of life, and everything we've built here, could be at risk. If The Heart of Haven isn't revitalized with Santa's magic, since Grizelda is clearly unable to right now, the entire town would be exposed to the human realm, and Santa's trip will be delayed too. He might not be able to finish without the symbiotic energy boost."

I gasp when his words sink in. This isn't just about decorations or a festival. It's about the very existence of this magical place, all the beings who call it home, and about four billion human children, who stand to be disappointed too. "There has to be something we can do," I say, surprising myself with how determined I am to fix this.

Frost looks at me with an arched eyebrow. "You want to help? Even though you've only just learned about all this?"

I nod. "I'm new to magic, but I'm good at problem-solving. There's always a solution if you look at things from a different angle."

For a moment, he seems to really see me for the first time. His eyes narrow as he studies me. "You're serious?"

I nod once more. "Absolutely. Just tell me what needs to be done."

He hesitates for a moment, then sighs. "Very well. There are three enchanted items we need to retrieve. They should help amplify the Heart's magic and stabilize it."

"Great," I say, pulling out my phone to take notes. "What are they?"

Frost blinks at my phone. "That won't work here. The magical interference—"

"Oh, right." I pocket the device and grab a nearby fallen twig. With a quick movement, I scratch a list in the snow. "Okay, go on."

He raises an eyebrow but continues. "First, we need the Christmas Star. It's hidden somewhere in my shop, but the shelves tend to...rearrange themselves, and it's probably lost in a labyrinth at the moment."

I jot down "Christmas Star—Frost's shop" in the snow. "Sounds like a scavenger hunt. What's next?"

"The Snow Globe of Eternal Winter. It's at 'Mystic Melodies,' but Heather Siren keeps it locked away. She's...particular about who handles it."

I add "Snow Globe—'Mystic Melodies'" to my list. "And the third item?"

"An Evergreen Branch from the oldest, most sacred tree in The Whispering Woods. The trees there are sentient and protective of their magic. It won't be easy to convince them to part with a branch, but they do like Throk, and your friend Candice has spoken to them. Not everyone can understand them."

I finish my list with "Evergreen Branch—Whispering Woods. Candice and Throk?" "All right, we have our targets. What's our timeline?"

He glances at the dimming Heart of Haven. "We have until midnight. If we don't stabilize the Heart by then, the barrier will fall, and Santa's portal won't open."

"No pressure," I mutter. "Okay, let's start with your shop. It's closest, and we know exactly what we're looking for."

Frost nods, a hint of surprise in his eyes. "You're taking charge quite efficiently for someone who just learned magic exists."

"I've known for a whole week now," I say with a forced smile and then shrug. "Magic or not, this is still a problem that needs solving. I'm good at that."

I stand, brushing snow from my knees as I think about the problems I've encountered in the real world, mostly because nothing has ever been a clear fit. I don't have time to dwell on that, but oddly, I feel in my element here, at least as we embark on our treasure hunt. "Lead the way to your shop, Frost."

Chapter 3

AS FROST AND I PREPARE to leave the town square, Grizelda steps forward, her wild mane of hair swaying with each movement. She raises her arms, palms facing outward, and a shimmering energy radiates from her fingertips. "I'll reinforce the barrier before you go," she says, her voice strained. "It should buy us some time."

The air around us crackles with magic, and I watch in awe as an iridescent dome materializes above the town. It's beautiful, like a soap bubble stretched across the sky, but as quickly as it appears, it flickers and fades.

Grizelda's face contorts in concentration. She tries again, her hands trembling with effort. The barrier flashes once more, but it's weaker this time, barely visible before it dissipates entirely.

"Something's wrong," whispers Frost, currently orange eyes wide with concern.

Suddenly, the witch's knees buckle. She sways on her feet, her eyes rolling back in her head. Atlas, her towering troll husband, rushes forward with surprising agility for someone his size. He catches her just before she hits the ground, cradling her gently in his massive arms.

"Grizelda?" Atlas's deep voice rumbles with worry. "What's happening?"

The crowd around us murmurs anxiously. I spot Sage, the elderly elf librarian I met a couple of days ago, pushing his way through. His long silver braid swings behind him as he hurries to Grizelda's side.

"Let me see her," he says, adjusting the glasses perched on his pointed ears. He places a wrinkled hand on Grizelda's forehead and closes his eyes. A soft golden glow emanates from his palm.

After a moment, his eyes snap open. "It's magical burnout. The strain of maintaining the barrier, combined with her pregnancy, has depleted her magical reserves."

Atlas cradles Grizelda closer, seeming to droop with worry. "Can you help her?"

Sage shakes his head. "My healing abilities are limited, but I know where to find the information we need." Without another word, he vanishes in a puff of smoke, leaving behind a trail of floating bookmarks.

The town square falls silent, save for Grizelda's labored breathing. Frost shifts nervously beside me, his hair frosting over at the tips. I want to reach out and comfort him, but I'm not sure how.

Seconds later, Sage reappears, clutching a massive leather-bound tome. He flips through the pages with practiced ease, muttering under his breath.

"Ah, here it is," he says finally. "'Magical Burnout In Pregnant Witches.' The treatment is simple, but crucial." He looks up at Atlas. "She needs rest. Complete magical rest. No spells, no potion-making, and nothing that could tax her magical core for at least a week."

Atlas nods solemnly. "I'll make sure she rests."

Grizelda stirs in his arms, her eyelids fluttering open. "No," she protests weakly. "The barrier... The town needs me."

"The town needs you healthy," says Atlas firmly. "We'll find another way to protect Evershift Haven."

Frost steps forward, his face set with determination. "That's where we come in," he says, gesturing to me. "We'll find the artifacts and stabilize the Heart of Haven. You focus on getting better, Grizelda."

She looks like she wants to argue, but exhaustion wins out. She nods weakly, then turns her gaze to me. "Be careful. The magic in this town can be unpredictable, especially now."

I swallow hard. "We will be."

As Atlas carries Grizelda a few feet away, whispered conversations break out among the townspeople. Frost turns to me, his expression revealing worry and resolution. "We should get moving," he says. "Time is running out, and without Grizelda to maintain the barrier, who knows what might happen?"

I nod, trying to ignore the flutter of nerves in my stomach. As Frost and I prepare to leave, a sudden change in the atmosphere draws my attention back to the Heart of Haven. The ancient oak tree, usually radiating a warm, golden glow, now flickers erratically. Its leaves rustle in distress, despite the lack of wind.

"Frost, look," I say, pointing at the tree.

He turns, his silver-white braid swinging with the motion. His eyes, now periwinkle, widen. "This isn't good."

The tree's branches wave wildly, as if trying to communicate. Its glow dims further, shifting to a sickly yellow hue. It's almost as if the tree is reacting to the news of Grizelda's condition.

"Is it...sentient?" I ask, unable to tear my gaze from the unsettling sight.

He nods solemnly. "In a way, yes. The Heart of Haven is deeply connected to the town and its inhabitants. Grizelda's illness must be affecting it more than we realized."

Without thinking, I step closer to the tree. Its distress tugs at something deep within me, an inexplicable urge to offer comfort. I reach out, my hand hovering over the rough bark.

"Evony, wait—" he says, but I've already made contact.

The moment my fingers touch the tree, a strange sensation courses through me. It's like a current of energy, warm and tingling, flowing from the tree into my body and back again. The erratic flickering of the Heart's glow steadies, if only for a moment. I gasp, pulling away my hand. The connection breaks, and the tree resumes its distressed state, though perhaps not as severely as before.

"What was that?" I ask, flexing my fingers. They still tingle with residual energy.

Frost stares at me, his expression surprised and something else I can't quite identify. "I'm not sure," he says slowly. "It seemed like you were able to calm the Heart, even if only briefly."

I shake my head, trying to clear the fog that's settled over my thoughts. My ears tingle strangely, and I resist the urge to reach up and touch them. "It must be all this magic in the air," I say, forcing a laugh. "I'm not used to it. I'm just a human, after all. I'm sure I'll acclimate eventually."

Frost opens his mouth as if to argue, then closes it again. He studies me for a long moment before speaking. "Perhaps," he says, though he doesn't sound convinced. "We should get moving. Time is of the essence."

I nod, grateful for the change of subject. "Right. You said we need to go to your shop first?"

"Yes, for the Christmas Star. It's our best bet for stabilizing the Heart quickly."

I can't shake the lingering sensation from my encounter with the Heart of Haven. It felt...familiar, somehow. Like reconnecting with an old friend.

I push aside the thought. There's no time for such fanciful notions. We have a town to save, and apparently, only until midnight to do it. Still, I linger with Frost, watching the townsfolk debate how to manage without Grizelda. Their voices rise and fall with worry and half-formed plans.

"We'll need volunteers for the protection spells," says Sage, his spectacles glinting in the fading light. "I can teach the basics, but it will take several of us working in shifts."

Atlas, still cradling Grizelda, nods solemnly. "I'll organize a rotation. We have enough magical beings to cover the essentials."

"What about the seasonal transitions?" asks Bella, wringing her hands. "Grizelda always oversees those."

Heather, the mermaid who owns "Mystic Melodies," and is currently in her fully human form, raises her hand. "I can handle the water-based elements. The lake, the fountains—those should be manageable."

"And I'll take care of the plant life," says the treant, Oakhart, his bark-like skin creaking as he shifts. "The Whispering Woods will help spread the word to the rest of the flora."

I watch in amazement as the townspeople rally, each offering their unique skills to fill the void left by Grizelda's absence. It's touching, really, how this eclectic community comes together in a crisis.

Frost leans close, his cool breath tickling my ear. "We need to go," he whispers. "Time's running out."

I nod, realizing how long we've been standing here. We slip away from the crowd, their voices fading as we hurry down the cobblestone street toward Frost's shop.

Chapter 4

I PUSH OPEN THE DOOR to "Frost's Festive Finds," and a wave of peppermint and pine washes over me. The shop's interior is a kaleidoscope of Christmas colors, but something's off. The shelves aren't neatly arranged as I remember from my first visit. Instead, they float in midair, shifting and rearranging themselves like a giant 3D puzzle.

"This is new," I say, eyeing the moving shelves warily.

"Not entirely. The shelves often rearrange themselves, but not to this extent." Frost steps in behind me, eyeing the chaos. "The Heart's instability is affecting the shop's magic. We'll need to navigate carefully."

I scan the room, trying to spot the Christmas Star among the chaos. "Any idea where you last saw it?"

"It should be on the top shelf near the back," he says while looking around the room. "But with everything moving..."

A shelf zooms past us, narrowly missing my head. I duck instinctively. "Great. So we're looking for a needle in a haystack, and the haystack is trying to decapitate us."

Frost's lips twitch, almost smiling. "Your human sayings are quite amusing. Shall we begin our search?"

I nod, stepping forward cautiously. A path seems to open up between two shelves, but as soon as I move toward it, they slam together. I jump back, bumping into Frost. He steadies me with his hands on my hips, creating a strange tingle where we touch.

"Perhaps we should approach this methodically," he says. "I'll start on the left, and you take the right. We'll work our way to the center."

I raise an eyebrow. "Methodically? In this chaos? We don't have time for that. We need to grab that star before midnight."

"Patience is key in magical endeavors." He sniffs. "Rushing could lead to mistakes."

I roll my eyes. "And being too cautious could mean we don't find it at all." As an accountant, it's odd for me to argue that we should rush in, but the situation is extraordinary. "I get that you're the expert on magic here, but I'm pretty good at problem-solving. How about we try it my way first?"

Without waiting for an answer, I dart forward, ducking under a low-hanging shelf and weaving between two others. Frost calls out behind me, but I'm focused on the task at hand. I spot a glimmer of gold near the back of the shop and make a beeline for it.

As I reach for the star, a shelf swoops down, forcing me to roll out of the way. I end up behind a display of nutcrackers, their painted eyes seeming to follow me.

"Evony?" Frost appears beside me, his silver hair slightly disheveled. "Are you all right?"

"I'm fine." I brush off my clothes. "I think I saw the star over there."

He gives me a stern look. "We need to work together on this. The shop's magic is unpredictable right now."

I'm about to argue when I notice something odd. The shelves seem to be moving in a pattern, almost like... "It's a dance," I whisper.

"What?"

I grab Frost's hand without thinking. "Look. The shelves are moving like they're dancing. If we can figure out the rhythm..."

His eyes widen in understanding. He squeezes my hand, and that strange tingle returns. "Brilliant observation, Evony. Shall we dance?"

Together, we start moving through the shop, stepping in time with the shelves' movements. It's like a complicated waltz, with Frost leading and me following his cues. We weave between floating displays, duck under swinging signs, and twirl past precarious stacks of gift boxes.

When we near the back of the shop, I spot the star again. "There." I point with my free hand.

Frost nods, guiding us closer. Just as we're about to reach it, a group of small, fluffy creatures hop into view. They look like a cross between rabbits and cotton balls, with big, innocent eyes.

Frost stiffens. "Floffels," he whispers, his voice tense. "Don't make any sudden moves."

I stare at the adorable creatures. "They're so cute. What's the problem?"

As if in answer, one of the floffels opens its mouth, revealing rows of razor-sharp teeth. The others follow suit, their cute facade melting away as they advance toward us.

Frost's grip on my hand tightens. "Run."

We turn and sprint through the maze of shelves, the floffels hopping after us with surprising speed. Frost pulls me along, his touch unexpectedly warm despite his icy appearance. We dodge and weave, barely staying ahead of the snapping floffels.

"There." Frost points to a sliver of light between two shelves. We dive through the gap just as it starts to close, leaving the floffels on the other side.

We stand there, catching our breath, and still holding hands. I look up at Frost, noticing how the light catches in his silver hair. "So," I say between pants, "Cute and fluffy until they show their teeth, huh?"

Frost chuckles, a warm sound that seems at odds with his cool exterior. "Indeed. Floffels are quite the menace when agitated. Are you all right?"

I nod, suddenly very aware that we're still holding hands. I reluctantly let go, missing the warmth immediately. "I'm fine, but we still need to get that star." As I turn to go back the way we came, I realize we aren't in his shop any longer.

A vast expanse of shimmering ice caverns stretches before us, their crystalline walls refracting light in dazzling patterns. The air is crisp and clean, with a hint of mint that tickles my nose.

"Wow," I say, eyes wide as I take in the alien landscape. "Where are we?"

Frost steps closer, resting his hand lightly on my back to steady me. "A pocket dimension. This must be where the floffels originated."

The cavern walls pulse with an otherworldly blue light, casting dancing shadows across the icy floor. Stalactites of pure ice hang from the ceiling like frozen chandeliers, and in the distance, I hear the faint tinkling of what sounds like wind chimes.

"It's beautiful." I turn to look at Frost, struck by how the ethereal light makes his silver hair shimmer. Our gazes meet, and for a second, the world seems to stand still.

His hand on my back feels warm despite our frigid surroundings. He leans in slightly, and I find myself moving closer too. Our lips are just inches apart when a loud squeak breaks the spell.

We jump apart, spinning to face the source of the noise. A floffel, easily twice the size of the ones we encountered in the shop, stands before us. Its fluffy body quivers with what I can only assume is rage, and its mouth opens to reveal rows of razor-sharp teeth. It screams protective mama bear...er, floffel...vibes. I'd bet the littles we encountered in Frost's shop belong to this big, angry mother, looking for her babies.

"Time to go," he says, grabbing my hand.

We dash back through the sliver of light, tumbling into the questionable safety of Frost's shop. The giant floffel's angry squeaks echo behind us and is getting closer.

Frost doesn't waste a second. He raises his hands, and a swirling vortex of snow appears in the center of the room. The floffels, caught off-guard, are swept up into the miniature blizzard. With a final gesture, Frost directs the snow tornado back through the rapidly closing portal.

As the last floffel disappears, he slumps against a nearby shelf, his face pale and drawn. "That was more taxing than anticipated," he says, his voice weak.

I rush to his side, placing a hand on his shoulder. "Are you okay?"

The moment my fingers make contact, a spark of energy seems to pass between us. Frost straightens up, color returning to his cheeks. He blinks in surprise, looking from my hand to my face.

"I'm...fine," he says slowly, a strange expression crossing his features. "Better than fine, actually. How did you do that? Only another fae should be able to boost my energy."

I quickly pull away my hand, suddenly self-conscious. "I didn't do anything. You must have just needed a moment to recover."

Frost opens his mouth as if to argue, then closes it again. An awkward silence falls between us, and I think about our almost-kiss in the ice cavern. My cheeks heat up at the memory. "We should probably get back to looking for that star," I say, desperate to break the tension. "The Heart of Haven isn't going to fix itself."

Frost nods, seemingly grateful for the change of subject. "Yes, of course. The star should be easier to find now that the floffels are gone."

We begin our search anew, carefully navigating the still-floating shelves. As we work, I sneak glances at Frost. That moment in the ice cavern... Was it just the stress of the situation? The alien beauty of our surroundings? Or was there something more between us?

I shake my head, trying to focus on the task at hand. We have a town to save. Whatever I think I felt—whatever almost happened—will have to wait. Right now, finding that star is all that matters.

I weave through the maze of floating shelves, scanning for any sign of the Christmas Star. Frost follows close behind. The shop's chaos has settled somewhat, but the shelves still drift lazily through the air, occasionally bumping into each other with soft chimes.

"There." I point to a glimmer of gold nestled between two ornament-laden shelves. The Christmas Star hovers above a pedestal, its light flickering erratically.

Frost's eyes widen. "Good eye, Evony. We need to approach carefully. The star's magic is unstable."

We inch forward, dodging a rogue shelf that swoops past. As we near the pedestal, I feel a strange pull, like an invisible thread tugging at my core. The star's light pulses in sync with my heartbeat.

"Evony, wait—" Frost starts, but I'm already reaching out.

My fingers brush the star's surface, and a jolt of energy surges through me. The shop around us fades away, replaced by a swirling vortex of light and color. Images flash before my eyes—a snow-covered forest, a group of elves crafting toys, and a sleigh soaring through the night sky.

I gasp, overwhelmed by the visions. Instinctively, I focus on steadying my breathing, imagining roots growing from my feet into the ground. To my surprise, the chaotic energy begins to calm. The star's erratic flickering slows, settling into a steady, warm glow.

The vortex dissipates, and I'm back in Frost's shop. The star rests in my palm, its light now strong and constant. I look up to see him staring at me, eyes wide with astonishment.

"How did you do that?"

I shake my head, still processing what just happened. "I... I don't know. It just felt right."

He takes a step closer. "Do you realize what you've done? You've stabilized an ancient magical artifact with no training. That's extraordinary."

Heat rises to my cheeks under his scrutiny. "I'm sure it's nothing. Maybe the star just needed a human touch or something."

Frost shakes his head. "No, it's more than that. You have a gift. A connection to magic that I've rarely seen in humans."

I open my mouth to protest, but the words die on my tongue. How can I deny what just happened? The visions and the energy coursing through me were unlike anything I've ever experienced.

Frost gently takes the star from my hand, brushing his fingers against mine. That same spark of energy passes between us, and his eyes widen slightly. He places the star in a velvet pouch, then turns back to me.

"Thank you, Evony," he says, his voice softer than I've ever heard it. "Your help has been invaluable."

The warmth in his tone makes me tremble. I'm abruptly lost in his gaze, noticing flecks of silver in his eyes that are currently a deep purple. The air between us feels charged, like the moment before lightning strikes.

I clear my throat, breaking the spell. "We should probably get going. We still have two more items to find, right?"

He blinks, as if coming out of a trance. "Yes, of course. The Snow Globe of Eternal Winter awaits us at 'Mystic Melodies.'"

As we make our way out of the shop, I replay the moment in my mind. The way Frost looked at me, and the awe in his voice, stirs something deep within me, a longing I didn't know I had.

Too bad there's no time for that now. We have a town to save, and apparently, I have some latent magical ability to figure out. Just another day in Evershift Haven, I suppose.

Chapter 5

I STEP INTO "MYSTIC Melodies," and tinkling wind chimes announce our arrival. The shop's interior is a kaleidoscope of colors and sounds, with instruments of all shapes and sizes lining the walls and floating in mid-air. Frost follows close behind, his cool presence a stark contrast to the warm, vibrant atmosphere of the store.

"Hello?" I call out, my voice echoing through the shop. "Anyone here?"

A flash of bright feathers catches my eye, and suddenly, a large, colorful parrot swoops down from a high perch, landing on a nearby display case. His iridescent plumage shimmers in the soft light of the shop.

"Hmm..." The parrot squawks, cocking his head to the side. "What do we have here? A frosty fellow and a...hmm, interesting spark."

I blink, taken aback by the talking bird. "Did that parrot just—"

"Speak? Of course I did, darling," interrupts the parrot, ruffling his feathers. "The name's Paulie, and I'm not your average squawker."

Frost steps forward, his expression serious. "Paulie, we need the Snow Globe of Eternal Winter. It's urgent."

Paulie hops from one foot to the other, his beady eyes fixed on me. "Urgent, you say? Isn't that exciting, but tell me, frosty one, have you noticed anything unusual about your companion here?"

I shift uncomfortably under the bird's scrutiny. "We don't have time for games. The Heart of Haven is failing, and we need that snow globe."

"Oh, ho." Paulie cackles, spreading his wings. "She's got fire, this one. Or should I say...magic?"

"What are you talking about?" I ask, my patience wearing thin.

He ignores my question, instead addressing Frost. "You feel it too, don't you? That hidden spark. It's quite electrifying."

Frost glances at me, his currently-navy eyes scrunched by a frown. There's a question in his gaze that makes my palms sweaty.

"Enough riddles," says Frost, turning back to Paulie. "Will you give us the snow globe or not?"

The parrot preens, clearly enjoying our frustration. "Where's the fun in just handing it over? I propose a challenge. Solve my riddle, and the snow globe is yours."

I sigh, running a hand through my curls, which are starting to tangle. "Fine. What's your riddle?"

Paulie clears his throat dramatically. "I am not alive, but I grow. I don't have lungs, but I need air. I don't have a mouth, but water kills me. What am I?"

I furrow my brow, considering the clues. Not alive but grows, needs air, water kills it... "Fire," I say confidently. "The answer is fire."

Paulie's eyes widen in surprise. "Aren't you the clever one? Perhaps that hidden spark of yours is brighter than I thought."

"What do you mean by 'hidden spark?'" I demand, growing frustrated with the bird's cryptic comments.

The parrot cocks his head, regarding me with an almost pitying look. "Oh, sweetie. You really don't know, do you? There's magic in you, clear as day to those who can see it. Right, Frosted Flake?"

Frost shifts uncomfortably beside me. "Paulie, that's enough. We solved your riddle. Give us the snow globe."

But I'm not ready to let this go. "Frost? What is he talking about?"

He hesitates. "I... I've sensed something different about you since we met. A kind of energy, but now's not the time to discuss it. We need to focus on saving Evershift Haven."

Paulie cackles again. "Oh, this is too good. The elf can see it, but the girl's in denial. Trust me, honey, that spark in you is just waiting to ignite. You might want to look into that elvish grandmother of yours."

"Elvish grandmother?" I repeat, my mind reeling. "That's impossible. My family is completely normal."

"Is it now?" Paulie asks, tone dripping with sarcasm. "I suppose those pointed ears you're sprouting are just a fashion statement, then?"

My hands fly to my ears, and to my shock, I feel the slightest point at the tips. "What's happening to me?"

Frost places a comforting hand on my shoulder, causing a jolt of electricity from his touch. "We'll figure this out, but right now, we need that snow globe."

I nod, trying to push aside the whirlwind of questions in my mind. "Right. The snow globe. Paulie, we solved your riddle. Please, give us the Snow Globe of Eternal Winter."

Paulie cackles, flapping his wings dramatically. "Congratulations, clever ones. You've earned passage to the next challenge. Prepare yourselves for a magical obstacle course like no other."

"Next challenge? You said—" Being swallowed in a flash of light distracts me from finishing the sentence. In a blink, we're transported to a whimsical landscape. Floating platforms hover in the air, connected by shimmering bridges of light. Colorful creatures dart between the platforms, shifting and changing their forms as they move.

"This is certainly different," I say, taking in our new surroundings.

Frost nods, also scanning the area. "We need to be careful. These pocket dimensions can be unpredictable."

"I hope there are no floffels."

We start making our way across the first bridge, its surface rippling beneath our feet like water. When we reach the first platform, a small, imp-like creature appears before us.

"Riddle me this," it squeaks, its voice high-pitched and mischievous. "I have cities, but no houses. I have mountains, but no trees. I have water, but no fish. What am I?"

I furrow my brow, considering the clues. "A map." I respond with confidence.

The imp grins, revealing pointed teeth. "Correct. Proceed, clever ones."

We continue through the course, solving riddles and navigating increasingly bizarre obstacles. At one point, we have to cross a chasm by stepping on musical notes that appear in the air, each one playing a different tone when we touch it.

Midway through the course, we reach a platform that seems to pulse with energy. As soon as we step onto it, a shimmering bubble forms around us, lifting us high into the air. "What's happening?" I ask, pressing my hands against the translucent surface. It's surprisingly sturdy.

Frost frowns, tracing patterns on the bubble's interior. "It seems the enchantment has glitched. We're trapped until I can figure out how to dispel it."

I turn to face him, suddenly aware of how close we are in this confined space. We touch, and a jolt of electricity runs through me. "So," I say, trying to keep my voice steady, "I guess we have some time to kill."

His lips quirk into a small smile. "It appears so. Perhaps we could use this opportunity to...talk?"

I raise an eyebrow. "Talk? About what?"

He takes a deep breath. "About what Paulie said. About the magic within you."

I shake my head, laughing nervously. "That's ridiculous. I'm just a normal human. There's nothing magical about me."

He reaches out, brushing his cool fingers against my cheek. "I've sensed it since the moment we met. There's something extraordinary about you."

My heart races at his touch. "How is that possible? My family is completely ordinary."

He shrugs. "Magic can sometimes skip generations. It's possible you have magical ancestry of which you're unaware."

I lean closer to him, drawn by an invisible force. "And what if it's true? What does that mean for me?"

His eyes become bright pink as his gaze drops to my lips. "It means you belong in our world, Evony. In Evershift Haven. With..."

He trails off, but I understand what he's not saying. With him.

I close the distance between us, pressing my lips to his. The kiss is electric, sending sparks of magic coursing through my body. Frost responds with intensity, wrapping his arms around me as he deepens the kiss.

The bubble around us pulses with energy, responding to our connection. Colors swirl in the air, creating a dazzling light show.

When we finally break apart, both breathless, he looks at me with a mixture of desire and uncertainty. "I... I haven't allowed myself to feel this way in a very long time."

I smile, running my fingers through his silver-white hair. "Maybe it's time to start."

He hesitates for a moment, then pulls me close, capturing my lips in a passionate kiss. The bubble around us glows brighter, enveloping us in a cocoon of light and magic. I lose myself in the sensation, letting go of all doubt and fear.

I weave my hand into the intricate braid confining his hair, loosening a few silvery-white strands in the process. He shudders when I brush my fingertips over his ears. They're elongated and pointed, and he shivers when I stroke the pointed tips. "Do you like that?" I ask.

His eyelids flutter shut as he nods. "Yes. Very much."

I continue exploring his sensitive ears, delighting in the sounds he makes as I caress them. He leans into my touch, his breathing growing ragged.

"Are your ears always this sensitive?"

He shakes his head. "No. Only when I'm aroused."

I grin, feeling bolder. "Let's see what else we can do to make you even more aroused."

I move my hands lower, trailing them down his chest and abdomen, longing to feel the skin underneath. He's wearing a white button-down shirt and a green velvet vest with a green and gold tie. I slowly undo the buttons of his vest before moving on to his shirt. When I get to the last one, I push aside the fabric and gasp at the sight of his bare chest.

He's muscular and toned, with pale skin that seems to glow in the dim light of the bubble. I trace my fingers over his defined abs, marveling at the smoothness of his skin. He inhales sharply as I explore his body, his muscles tensing under my touch.

"You're beautiful," I whisper, leaning forward to press a kiss to his collarbone.

He groans softly, tilting his head back as I trail kisses down his neck and across his chest. "So are you," he says hoarsely.

I look up at him, smiling mischievously. "Why don't you show me how beautiful you think I am?"

He doesn't hesitate, pulling me into another passionate kiss while tugging at the hem of my shirt. We break apart long enough for him to pull it over my head, tossing it aside. He deftly unclasps my bra, freeing my breasts.

He cups them gently, brushing his thumbs over my nipples. I moan, arching into his touch. "Oh, yes."

He continues teasing my dark nipples until they're hard peaks, then bends down to take one into his mouth. I cry out, tangling my fingers in his hair as he sucks and licks my sensitive flesh. "More," I beg. "Please, Frost."

He obliges, switching to my other breast while sliding a hand down my stomach and into my leggings. He finds my clit easily, pressing down on it with his thumb and gliding over the sensitive nub through the silk of my white panties. Thank goodness I'm not wearing granny panties today. They aren't sexy—just hip-hugging briefs—but they aren't ginormous either.

I grind against his hand, desperate for more friction. He chuckles, releasing my nipple with a wet pop. "I'll give you more, Evony, but first, I want these off." He hooks his fingers into the waistband of my pants and tugs them down. I help him remove them after sliding out of my sneakers, kicking them away impatiently.

He kneels before me, gazing up at me with lust-filled eyes now a simmering deep purple shade. "Now, let's see what we have here." He slides my panties down my legs, exposing my slick folds. He runs a finger through my pussy lips, gathering some of my juices before bringing it to his mouth. He closes his eyelids, savoring the taste of me. "Delicious," he whispers.

My cheeks flush hotly as he drops to his knees. The bubble flexes around his new position, still encompassing us. Escaping is a problem to solve for future-us. Right now, I need him to touch me again.

He spreads my thighs wide, burying his face between them. I cry out as he laps at my slit, tracing circles around my clit with his tongue. He teases me mercilessly, alternating between slow, broad strokes and quick flicks of his tongue. My hips buck involuntarily each time he hits my clit just right, sending shivers of pleasure through my entire body.

"Frost." I gasp, gripping his hair tightly. "That feels so good."

He hums in agreement, continuing his ministrations. I'm already close to coming when he presses his tongue flat against my clit and begins vibrating it rapidly. I explode instantly, screaming his name as I ride out my orgasm.

He pulls back slightly, grinning up at me. "Did you like that?"

I nod weakly, struggling to catch my breath. "Yes...very much."

He stands up, wiping his mouth with the back of his hand. "Good." He draws out the word as he reaches for me, pulling me into his arms. "Because I'm not done with you yet."

The bubble won't expand enough for us to lie down, but the walls are sturdy enough to allow me to slump backward against one. He lifts me effortlessly, wrapping my legs around his waist. His cock strains against his pants, pressing against my pussy, and reach down to free his cock, stroking it slowly.

"Evony..."

I smile wickedly, running my thumb over the tip. "What is it, Frost? Do you want something?"

His eyes flash with desire. "You know what I want."

I continue stroking him, enjoying the feeling of power it gives me. "Tell me."

He grits his teeth, thrusting into my hand. "I want to join with you."

My eyes widen as I stroke down his shaft, discovering elves are anatomically different from human men. There are two ridges on the underside of his cock, which seem to pulse and throb under my touch. "Oh, my god," I whisper. "You're double-ridged."

He smirks. "Is that a problem?"

I shake my head vigorously. "Not at all. Just surprised."

He leans forward, capturing my lips in a fierce kiss as I explore further—discovering he also has no testicles. They must be inside him. Without that impediment, I can grasp the full base, but my fingers don't reach. He's tapered too. "This is intriguing and a little alarming," I say with a hitch in my breathing.

"Alarming?" His voice is husky with arousal.

"How big are you?"

He laughs softly. "Bigger than any human man."

I swallow hard, wondering how I'll fit him inside me. "Are you going to hurt me?"

He shakes his head. "No, Evony. I'd never hurt you."

I look into his eyes, searching for the truth. "Promise?"

He nods solemnly. "I promise."

I take a deep breath, steeling myself for what's about to happen. "Okay, then. Let's do this."

He smiles, kissing me gently. "Relax. There's no rush."

I nod, trying to calm my racing heart. "Right. No rush." Except we have to find the magical items to reinforce The Heart of Haven before midnight, but...

I lose the train of thought when he lifts my thigh to wrap my leg higher around him, opening me more to his cock. He slides the tip through my folds, coating himself in my wetness. I moan softly as he rubs against my clit, sending ripples of pleasure through me.

"Do you want me, Evony?" he asks with desire.

I nod eagerly. "Yes, Frost. I want you."

He grins, positioning himself at my entrance. "Then take me."

With those words, he pushes into me slowly, allowing me to adjust to his size. I gasp as he stretches me open, filling me completely. It's almost overwhelming, but in a delicious way. I've never felt so full before, and I love it.

As he bottoms out, I let out a long sigh of satisfaction. "You feel amazing."

He chuckles. "So do you."

We stay like that for a moment, savoring the connection between us. Then he begins to move, thrusting in and out of me with slow, deliberate strokes. My body responds instantly, arching toward him as I seek more friction. He obliges, picking up the pace until he's pounding into me with wild abandon. I cling to him, riding the waves of ecstasy that wash over me with every thrust. It feels incredible, and I never want it to end.

Where he was once cool and aloof, he burns now. He's still icy in a magical way, but it's the kind of ice that feels warm to the touch, not cold. As he fucks me, I feel like I'm melting into him, becoming part of him. It's both terrifying and exhilarating, and I can't get enough.

I dig my nails into his back, urging him on. "Harder," I beg. "Please, Frost. More."

He growls, gripping my hips tightly as he slams into me. The force of his thrusts sends shock-waves through my entire body, and I cry out in pleasure. I'm so close to the edge, teetering on the brink of oblivion. All it takes is one final push to send me tumbling over the precipice into blissful release as I sag back against the bubble wall.

Frost follows soon after, burying himself deep inside me as he comes with a roar. We collapse together against the bubble wall, panting and spent. For a few moments, there's only silence as we catch our breath.

Then Frost speaks. "Evony..."

I turn to face him, unable to hide the smile on my face. "Yes?"

His expression is serious, but there's a glimmer of amusement in his eyes. "That was...unexpected."

I laugh softly. "It certainly was."

He pauses, considering his next words carefully. "Would you be amenable to doing it again sometime?"

My grin widens. "Absolutely."

He gives me a satisfied smirk.

As the afterglow fades, a thought occurs to me. I prop myself on one elbow against the bubble wall. "Can elves and humans... I mean, is it possible for them to..."

He seems to understand my unfinished question. "To conceive? Yes, it's possible. Though rare."

I think about Grizelda, so ill from her magical pregnancy. "And would it be dangerous? Like with Grizelda?"

He shakes his head. "Grizelda's situation is unique. A witch carrying a child who is half mountain troll is far more magically taxing than an elf-human pregnancy would be."

His words make me pause, and I realize my ears are tingling again. I reach up to touch them. To my shock, they feel longer and even pointier than before. "Frost," I say, my voice shaking slightly, "I think Paulie might have been right about my heritage."

He sits up, examining my ears with a mixture of surprise and wonder. "It appears the parrot was more perceptive than we gave him credit for. I believe you may indeed have elven ancestry."

I stare at him, my mind reeling with the implications. "But what does this mean? For me? For us?"

Frost takes my hand, intertwining our fingers. "It means your adventure in Evershift Haven is only just beginning."

I gaze at him, my heart still racing from our intimate encounter. The iridescent bubble surrounding us pulses with magical energy, a constant reminder of our predicament. "We need to figure out how to get out of here," I say, running my fingers through my tousled locks.

He nods, his silver-white braid disheveled now. "You're right. There must be another riddle or puzzle to solve."

We examine the bubble's surface, searching for clues. As my hand brushes against it, I notice a faint shimmer. Leaning closer, I see words etched in glowing script.

"To break free from this magical sphere,

Unite your strengths, both far and near.
One of logic, one of frost,
Combine your gifts or remain lost."

I read the riddle aloud, and he nods. "It's asking us to work together," he says. "Your logical mind and my frost magic."

"But how?" I ask, frowning. "I don't have any magical abilities."

Frost takes my hand. "You do. You just haven't fully awakened them yet. Trust your instincts."

I close my eyes, focusing on the energy I can sense humming around us. "Okay," I say, taking a deep breath. "Let's try something."

I place my palm against the bubble's surface, concentrating on the logical patterns I can discern in its magical structure. "Frost, can you channel your magic through me?"

He nods, positioning himself behind me and wrapping his arms around my waist. I gasp at a surge of icy power flowing through my body. It's exhilarating and terrifying all at once.

"Now," he whispers in my ear, "Visualize the bubble's structure breaking down. Use your analytical mind to find its weak points."

I focus intently, imagining the bubble as a complex equation. I can almost see the variables and constants, the intricate interplay of magical forces. With Frost's power augmenting my own nascent abilities, I begin to unravel the spell.

The bubble shimmers and vibrates. Cracks appear in its surface, spreading like a spider web. With a final push of combined energy, it shatters into a shower of glittering particles.

We fall, landing on a soft pile of cushions in a corner of "Mystic Melodies." The magical parrot, Paulie, flutters down to perch on a nearby shelf, looking entirely too pleased with himself. "Well done."

I blink, still processing what just happened. "Did we just...use magic together?"

Frost helps me to my feet, a proud smile on his face. "We did. You were incredible, Evony."

Before I can respond, a shimmering object catches my eye. On a pedestal near where we landed sits an exquisite snow globe. Inside, a miniature winter wonderland swirls with perpetual snowfall.

"The Snow Globe of Eternal Winter. We found it."

I reach out to take it, marveling at its delicate beauty. As my fingers close around the globe, I feel a surge of magical energy. The snowfall inside intensifies, and for a moment, I swear I can hear the faint tinkling of sleigh bells.

"It recognizes you," he says, his eyes wide with wonder. "Evony, I think this confirms it. You must have elven blood."

I stare at him as myriad emotions swirl inside me. "But how is that possible, Frost? My family is completely ordinary." I keep saying that, but is it true?

Paulie cackles, flapping his wings. "Ordinary? Ha. There's more to your family tree than meets the eye, dearie, but that's a mystery for another time."

I nod, tucking the snow globe safely into my bag. As we turn to leave "Mystic Melodies," Frost is watching me with a soft expression I've never seen before. He reaches out, tucking a stray lock of hair behind my ear—my slightly pointed ear, I realize with a start.

"You're amazing," he says softly. "I've never met anyone quite like you."

I blush. "You're pretty incredible yourself, Frost."

He smiles, a genuine, unguarded expression that makes my heart skip. Taking my hand, he leads me toward the shop's exit. "Come on," he says. "We have one more item to find."

Chapter 6

I STEP OUT INTO THE crisp winter air, crunching snow beneath my boots. Frost walks beside me, his silver-white hair shimmering in the moonlight. We're heading to meet Throk and Candice at Whispering Woods, but my mind races with everything that's happened since I arrived in Evershift Haven.

"You're awfully quiet," he says, his for-now pansy-colored irises revealing his concern. "Is everything all right?"

I nod, trying to find the right words. "Just...processing. This whole experience has been surreal." We've gotten so close so quickly that it's a little overwhelming for me. Most of my relationships have lasted no more than a few weeks, but I don't usually jump into bed—um, bubble—with guys on such short acquaintance though.

Frost chuckles, a sound like tinkling icicles. "I can imagine. It's not every day that a human discovers a magical town hidden between realities." He slants me a glance. "Or forms such an immediate connection..."

We walk in companionable silence for a few moments, our breath forming small clouds in the cold air. The streets of Evershift Haven are quiet at this hour, the magical shops closed for the night, and tension pervades the town. Everyone is clearly on edge, waiting to see if we succeed. Only the occasional glowing fairy light illuminates our path.

"Evony," he says softly, "There's something I need to tell you."

I turn to look at him, curious. "What is it?"

He takes a deep breath, looking at me. "I've dreamed about you for years."

I blink, not sure I heard him correctly. "You've...what?"

Frost runs a hand through his hair, leaving a trail of snowflakes and mussed hair escaping the braid in its wake. "I know it sounds crazy, but it's true. I've had visions of you in my dreams for as long as I can remember, always clearly in my future. When you were born about three decades ago, they increased in frequency and detail. When you appeared in Evershift Haven, I immediately knew who you were."

My mind reels. "Are you saying...you knew I was coming?"

He nods. "In a way, yes. I didn't know exactly when or how, but I knew you would arrive someday. You're my mate, Evony."

I stop walking to stare at him, mouth agape. "Your mate? Frost, we barely know each other. How can you possibly believe that?"

He turns to face me, his expression earnest. "In the fae world, we have something called dream prophecy. It's a rare gift that allows us to see glimpses of our future, particularly when it comes to our destined partners. I've seen you in my dreams for centuries, Evony. I've watched you grow up and seen snippets of your life in the human world. Over the past year, I've dreamed about you almost every night, so I knew you'd be coming soon, and now, here you are."

I shake my head, trying to process this information. "That's a lot to take in."

"I know. I don't expect you to feel the same way immediately. I've had years to come to terms with this, but for you, it's all new. I just wanted you to understand why I've been so drawn to you since you arrived."

I inhale deeply, and the cold air almost burns my lungs before I exhale. "I appreciate your honesty, Frost. I won't lie—I've felt a connection to you too, but this is moving so fast. I mean, magical prophecies? Destined mates? It's like something out of a fantasy novel."

He laughs softly. "Welcome to Evershift Haven, where fantasy becomes reality."

We start walking again, and I mull over his words. Despite the overwhelming nature of his revelation, I'm surprised to find I'm not entirely freaked out. There's a part of me that feels...right about this. Like a puzzle piece clicking into place. "So..." I say, breaking the silence. "These dreams you had about me. What exactly did you see?"

He gives me a sweet smile. "Oh, so many things. I saw you as a child, playing in a park near your home. I saw you in high school, winning a math competition. I saw you graduate college and start your first job as an accountant. Little snippets of your life, spread out over years. More than that, I saw snippets of our future together." His gaze softens. "There are two children in our future, both a perfect mix of us."

I stare at him, amazed. "That's...incredibly accurate, and a little freaky about the kid thing, but why me? I'm just a normal human. Or I was until I came here and discovered I have some kind of magical heritage."

Frost smiles. "You've never been 'just' anything. Your elven blood has always been a part of you, even if you didn't know it, and as for why you... That's the mystery of fate, isn't it?"

We walk in silence for a few moments while the snow falls gently around us. I'm struck by how comfortable I feel with Frost, despite the bombshell he just dropped on me. There's an ease between us that defies our short acquaintance. "Can I ask you something?"

"Anything."

"If you've known about me for so long, why didn't you try to find me in the human world?"

His expression turns serious. "It's forbidden for magical beings to interfere with the human world unless absolutely necessary. We have to let fate take its course. I knew you would find your way here when the time was right."

I nod, understanding. "And now that I'm here?"

He smiles, a hint of mischief in his eyes. "Now, I hope you'll give me a chance to court you properly. Dream visions are all well and good, but I want to get to know the real you."

I smile back. "I think I'd like that." I'm supposed to go home after Christmas, but the idea suddenly holds no appeal. I love my family and have friends there, along with enjoying my job, but I never seem to quite fit in either. Since coming to Evershift Haven, I haven't felt that low-grade compulsion to figure out my place in the scheme of things. I just seem to...fit.

Approaching the edge of the Whispering Woods, I see Throk and Candice waiting for us. Candice waves excitedly, her blonde hair glowing in the moonlight.

"There you are," she calls out. "We were starting to worry."

Throk nods in greeting, his massive form dwarfing Candice beside him. "Everything okay?"

I glance at Frost, who nods and smiles. "Yeah," I say, smiling. "Everything's great. So, what's this about talking trees?"

Candice grins. "Oh, you're going to love this. The Whispering Woods are amazing. The trees here are total gossips. They know everything that happens in Evershift Haven."

Throk chuckles, which sounds like a deep rumble emerging from his chest. "Just don't believe everything they tell you. Trees tend to exaggerate."

As we step into the woods, I hear a faint rustling that sounds almost like whispers. Frost takes my hand, sending warmth through me despite his cool touch.

"Ready for another magical adventure?" he asks, his eyes twinkling.

I squeeze his hand, feeling a surge of excitement. "Lead the way."

As we step into the Whispering Woods, a hush falls over our group. The trees tower above us, swaying their branches gently in a breeze I can't feel. There's an energy here, a presence that makes the hair on the back of my neck stand up.

Candice looks around, her eyes wide with excitement. "Oh, they're so happy to see us. Can you hear them, Evony?"

I shake my head, straining my ears. All I hear is the rustle of leaves. "I don't hear anything."

Candice looks disappointed but nods as Frost squeezes my hand. "It's okay. Most humans can't hear the trees. Just try to sense their mood."

I close my eyes, focusing on the energy around me. There's a welcoming feeling that washes over me. "They seem...friendly?"

Throk nods, his deep voice rumbling. "They are. The Whispering Woods love visitors."

We walk deeper into the forest, the path winding between ancient trunks. Suddenly, Candice stops, holding up a hand.

"What is it?" I ask.

She tilts her head, listening. "The trees say we can't go any farther. The sacred tree with the evergreen bough is off-limits."

Frost frowns. "We need that bough to save Evershift Haven. Can you explain our situation to them?"

Candice nods, then turns to face the nearest tree. She speaks in a language I don't understand, and her voice is melodic. The leaves rustle in response.

"What are they saying?" I whisper to Throk.

He chuckles. "They're reciting poetry. They're quite the romantics." He laughs again. "Their encouragement got Suzette to kiss me for the first time."

Candice's eyes widen abruptly, and she claps a hand over her mouth to stifle a giggle.

"What?" asks Frost, looking between Candice and Throk.

Throk grins. "The trees are teasing you and Evony about new love. They say your auras are intertwined." He wags his eyebrows suggestively. "In a certain way..."

Heat rushes to my cheeks. Frost coughs, looking anywhere but at me.

Candice turns to us, her expression revealing surprise and delight. "You two? Really? When did this happen?"

"It's...complicated," I mutter, not ready to explain Frost's dream prophecy. "We were trapped in a bubble, and..." I clear my throat. "I'll tell you later."

Frost clears his throat too. "Perhaps we should focus on the task at hand. Evony, why don't you try connecting with the trees?"

I blink at him. "Me? But I can't even hear them."

"Trust your instincts," he says softly. "Your fae blood gives you a connection to nature. Just reach out with your feelings."

Candice seems startled to hear that about my heritage, and her questioning look prompts me to nod, silently indicating I'll tell her everything later.

With a deep breath, I step forward, placing my hand on the rough bark of the nearest tree. At first, I feel nothing but wood beneath my fingers. Then, slowly, warmth spreads through my palm. It's like a pulse, steady and strong. "I think I feel something," I whisper.

Frost moves behind me, placing his hands on my shoulders. "Good. Try to explain our situation. Tell them why we need the evergreen bough. Picture it in your mind."

I close my eyes, concentrating on the pulse beneath my hand. In my mind, I form an image of Evershift Haven, of the flickering Heart of Haven at its center. I think of the danger, of the barrier failing, and of the magic faltering in this wonderful place I've just discovered. Lastly, I imagine the disappointed children all over the world.

The pulse beneath my hand quickens. The leaves above us rustle more intensely, and a warm breeze caresses my face. When I think of the children, the pulse intensifies, and I almost hear the trees moan.

Candice gasps. "They're listening to you, Evony. They can sense your intentions."

Encouraged, I press on. I picture the evergreen bough, imagining its power helping to stabilize the Heart of Haven. I think of the joy and wonder I've experienced since arriving in this magical town, and how devastated I'd be to see the town at risk.

The forest around us seems to come alive. The trees sway, their branches reaching toward each other. A shower of golden leaves rains down on us.

"What's happening?" I ask, opening my eyes.

Throk's expression is one of awe. "They're clearing the path. You've earned their trust."

Sure enough, the trees in front of us are parting, revealing a narrow path that wasn't there before. At the end of it, I can see a massive tree, its trunk wider than any I've ever seen. One of its branches glows with a soft, green light.

Frost squeezes my shoulders. "You did it, Evony. That's the sacred tree with the evergreen bough."

I lean back against him, suddenly exhausted. "I can't believe that worked."

"I can," he says softly. "You're more powerful than you know."

Candice claps her hands. "This is amazing. The trees are so impressed. They say they haven't felt such devotion in centuries. They say you have strong fae magic."

I look at her, startled. "Fae magic? But I'm human."

Frost chuckles. "Mostly human, perhaps, but there's definitely fae blood in your veins, as everyone around you keeps saying."

I shake my head, trying to process this new information. "This is all happening so fast. First, I discover magic is real. Now I'm part fae?"

Throk pats my shoulder gently. "Welcome to Evershift Haven, where nothing is quite what it seems."

Frost takes my hand, his touch sending a spark through me. "We should get that evergreen bough to save our town and Christmas."

As we walk down the newly revealed path, the trees seem to whisper around us. I can't hear their words, but I can feel their approval and acceptance. I feel like I truly belong.

The sacred tree is just ahead, its presence both comforting and intimidating. The glowing branch seems to pulse with energy, calling to something deep within me. I approach the sacred tree, its massive trunk dwarfing everything around it. The enchanted evergreen branch glows with a soft, ethereal light, beckoning me closer. As I reach out, I feel a resistance, like an invisible barrier pushing against my hand.

"It's protecting itself," says Frost softly beside me. "You'll need to use your magic to harmonize with it."

How am I supposed to do that? I don't bother to ask. Acting on instinct, I focus on the energy flowing through me. It's still new and unfamiliar, but I can sense it thrumming just beneath my skin. I close my eyes, picturing the magic as a gentle stream flowing from my core to my fingertips.

The air around me shifts, and Candice gasps. "Oh, Evony, you're glowing."

I open my eyes to see a soft, golden light emanating from my skin. It pulses in rhythm with the glow of the evergreen branch. Slowly, the resistance fades, and I'm able to wrap my fingers around the branch.

As soon as I touch it, a surge of power rushes through me. It's overwhelming, like trying to contain an ocean in a teacup. My knees buckle, and I stagger backward.

Frost catches me in his strong arms, steadying me against his chest. "I've got you," he murmurs, his cool breath tickling my ear.

The world spins around me, the colors blurring and swirling. I cling to him, grateful for his solid presence. Gradually, the dizziness subsides, and I become acutely aware of how close we are. I turn in his arms, looking up into his now-cool blue eyes. While I watch, they darken to a stormy gray, filled with concern and something else—desire. The air between us crackles with energy.

Without a word, he bends down and captures my lips with his. The kiss is gentle at first, a soft brush of lips, but it quickly deepens. I melt into him, tangling my free hand in his hair. The braid is almost entirely unwoven now, so I wrap strands around my fist. The evergreen branch in my other hand pulses with energy, as if approving of our connection.

When we finally pull apart, I'm breathless. Frost's eyes are wide with wonder as they become a gentle green, and a dusting of snowflakes falls from his hair.

"Completely..." I trail off, unable to find the right words.

"Magical." He smiles at me, as if I'm the only person in the whole world besides him. I feel that too until a squeal of delight breaks the moment.

I turn to see Candice grinning from ear to ear, her hands clasped together in excitement. "I knew it," she says with a grin. "Oh, you two are so cute together."

I blush but can't stop smiling.

Throk stands beside Candice, looking approving and amused. "Looks like the Whispering Woods were right about your auras being intertwined." He bursts into laughter that rumbles through me with its intensity. My cheeks grow hotter, but I'm still smiling.

Frost chuckles, his arm still wrapped around my waist. "Indeed they were. The trees are rarely wrong about such things."

I look down at the evergreen branch in my hand, its glow now pulsing in sync with my own magical aura. At some point, it disconnected itself from the tree. "We should get this back to the Heart of Haven," I say, trying to focus on our mission despite the butterflies in my stomach.

Candice nods, her expression turning serious. "You're right. We don't have much time left."

As we prepare to leave the Whispering Woods, I hear a rustling sound. The trees around us seem to bend in, brushing their leaves against each other in a whispered conversation.

"What are they saying?" I ask, looking at Candice.

She tilts her head, listening intently. A smile spreads across her face. "They're giving you both their blessing and trust that you'll save our town and Christmas."

I glance at Frost, who looks both pleased and a little embarrassed. "No pressure or anything," he says with a wry smile.

We make our way out of the woods, and I'm amazed at how much my life has changed in such a short time. Just days ago, I was a normal human accountant. Now, I've learned I'm part fae, tentatively wielding magic, and apparently, destined for a happy future with the handsome fae by my side.

The path back to town seems shorter somehow, as if the woods themselves are eager for us to complete our mission. When we emerge from the tree line, I see the town square in the distance. The normally bustling area is eerily quiet, and the magical decorations hang limply.

"The Heart's magic is fading fast," says Frost, his voice tight with concern. "We need to hurry."

Chapter 7

I RUSH BACK TO THE town square with Frost, the three enchanted items clutched tightly in my arms. I'm nervous approaching the Heart of Haven, whose pulsing light grows fainter by the second. The townsfolk gather around, looking worried.

"We've got them," I say, holding up the Christmas Star, Snow Globe, and Evergreen Branch. "What do we do now?"

Frost takes the items from me. "We need to place them around the Heart in a triangular formation. Their combined magic should stabilize the barrier."

We hurry to position the artifacts. As soon as they're in place, a surge of energy ripples through the air. The Heart of Haven glows brighter, its light pulsing with renewed strength. For a moment, everything seems perfect.

Then, a loud crack echoes across the square. I look up to see fissures spreading across the dome of the magical barrier, like cracks in a massive eggshell.

"No," whispers Frost, his face pale. "It's not enough."

A strange sensation washes over me, like invisible tendrils of energy pulling at my very being. My skin tingles, and I gasp as an unfamiliar warmth spreads through my body.

"Evony?" Frost turns to me, concern etched on his face. "What's wrong?"

I struggle to find words as the sensation intensifies. "I don't know. It feels like...something's waking up inside me."

The pulling sensation grows stronger, and I stumble. Frost catches me, steadying me with his strong arms. "It's your fae heritage," he says softly. "The Heart is calling to your latent magic."

I shake my head, overwhelmed by the rush of sensations. "This can't be happening. I'm just an accountant from Chicago. I can't have magic."

Frost cups my face in his hands. "You're so much more than that. I've known it since the moment I first dreamed about you. Your magic has always been there, waiting to be awakened."

Another crack splits the air, and the barrier flickers ominously. Frost releases me and turns his attention back to the Heart of Haven. He raises his hands, channeling his own magic into the ancient tree. Streams of silvery light flow from his fingertips, enveloping the Heart in a shimmering cocoon.

"It's not enough." He grunts, strain evident in his voice. "The damage is too extensive. I can't hold it alone."

Without thinking, I step forward, placing my hands on the rough bark of the Heart. The pulling sensation intensifies, and I gasp as energy surges through me. It's overwhelming, terrifying, and exhilarating all at once.

"That's it, Evony. Let your magic flow. Connect with the Heart."

Every other magical creature in the town square also steps forward, joining hands. A swell of magic surrounds me, and I can feel it to my very depths. I close my eyes, focusing on the warmth spreading through my body. I imagine it as a river of light, flowing from my core and out through my hands. The bark beneath my fingers grows warm, then hot.

"It's working," shouts someone in the crowd. "Look at the barrier."

I open my eyes to see the cracks in the magical dome slowly closing, like reverse lightning streaking across the sky. The Heart of Haven pulses with renewed vigor, its light growing stronger by the second as the combined magic of the townspeople and the three items helps it heal.

As the last crack seals itself, the Celestial Clock Tower begins to chime. Midnight. We made it just in time.

The surge of energy subsides, and I sag against the Heart, suddenly exhausted. Frost is there in an instant, supporting me with his strong arms.

"We did it," he says, his voice filled with awe. "We saved Evershift Haven."

I look around at the cheering townsfolk, their faces lit with joy and relief. The reality of what just happened begins to sink in. "We... I used magic. *Real* magic."

Frost nods, a proud smile spreading across his face. "You did, and quite impressively, I might add."

"But how? I've never done anything like that before."

He brushes a strand of hair from my face. "Your fae heritage has always been a part of you, Evony. Coming to Evershift Haven and connecting with the Heart awakened what was already there."

I lean into his embrace, my mind reeling. Next time I see my grandmother, I'm going to have some questions for her.

The crowd around us erupts into cheers and applause. Candice rushes forward, enveloping me in a tight hug. "You finally found your 'thing,'" she says with a smile as her eyes shine with tears of joy.

I hug her back. "It feels like I have."

As the last echoes of the Celestial Clock Tower's chimes fade away, a hush falls over the crowd gathered in the town square. The newly repaired barrier shimmers with a soft, iridescent glow, casting a magical light over the faces of the townsfolk. I stand next to Frost, his arm still supporting me, as we catch our breath from the intense magical exertion. They're obviously waiting on something, and I assume it's Santa.

The rational part of me rejects the idea even as a low hum fills the air, growing louder with each passing second. The crowd parts, revealing a swirling vortex of red and green light materializing in the center of the square. My eyes widen as the portal expands, its edges sparkling with golden flecks.

"Is that...?" I whisper, unable to finish my question. It's crazy to think I'm actually going to see Santa Claus—that he's real.

Frost nods, a smile spreading across his face. "Santa's portal."

As if on cue, a sleigh and reindeer glide through the shimmering gateway. I immediately notice the driver in the sleigh. He's tall and broad-shouldered, with a flowing white beard and twinkling blue eyes. His red suit is trimmed with white fur, and he has a sack slung over his shoulder as the sleigh stops, and he gets down. There's no mistaking him—it's Santa Claus himself.

The crowd erupts in cheers and applause as Santa surveys the scene, his jolly laugh booming across the square. "Ho, ho, ho. What a welcome. It seems I've arrived just in time for some Christmas magic."

He strides toward us, each step leaving a trail of sparkling snowflakes in his wake. As he approaches, an external wave of warmth and joy washes over me, dispelling the lingering fatigue from my magical efforts.

"Ah, Frost, my boy," says Santa, clapping a hand on Frost's shoulder. "I see you've been busy, and who might this lovely young lady be?" He winks at me.

Frost's cheeks color slightly as he introduces me. "Santa, this is Evony Johnson. She helped save Evershift Haven."

Santa's eyes twinkle as he turns to me. "Evony, my dear, it's a pleasure to meet you. I've heard whispers of your arrival, but I must say, you've exceeded even my expectations." He winks again. "You were always on the nice list, you know."

I open my mouth to respond, but no words come out. I'm standing face-to-face with Santa Claus. The real Santa Claus. How does one even begin to process that?

Santa chuckles at my speechlessness. "Don't worry, dear. The first encounter with true Christmas magic can be quite overwhelming. Let's see what we can do about our dear Grizelda, shall we?"

He turns toward where Grizelda lies on a bed someone conjured or moved into the town square, likely at her insistence to oversee everything before she fell asleep. Atlas hovers anxiously by her side as the Christmas elf approaches them, reaching into his sack and pulling out a small, glowing orb. "This is the essence of pure Christmas joy. It should do the trick."

He gently places the orb on Grizelda's forehead. It dissolves into a shower of golden sparkles that envelop her body. The crowd watches in awe as color returns to Grizelda's cheeks, and her eyes flutter open.

"What...happened?" she asks, her voice weak but growing stronger by the second.

Atlas helps her sit up, tears of joy in his eyes. "You're okay, my love. Santa's here. He gave you extra magic to restore you faster."

Grizelda looks around, taking in the scene. Her eyes widen as they land on the Heart of Haven, once again glowing with its deep, healthy light. She looks immediate at me. "The Heart has connected to you, Evony."

I shift uncomfortably under her gaze, still not entirely used to the idea of having magical abilities. "I... I just wanted to help," I stammer.

Santa laughs heartily. "And help you did, Evony. Being connected to the Heart merely means you'll be contributing to the magic of the town."

"For as long as you stay," says Grizelda with a yawn. "The connection will sever when you leave."

"I..." I'm not sure how I feel about that. The idea of leaving sends a spasm through me, like a physical ache.

As if to emphasize her point, the barrier above us pulses with renewed energy, sending cascades of colorful light dancing across the sky. The townsfolk gasp and point as one of the branches sways toward my direction.

Santa turns back to Frost and me, a knowing smile on his face. "I must say, I'm particularly pleased to see the two of you working together so well. It warms my heart to see new love blossoming on Christmas."

My cheeks heat up, and I sneak a glance at Frost. He's looking at me with such tenderness that my pulse drums in my ears like a tribal rhythm.

"Now then," says Santa, "I believe we have some Christmas magic to share."

The crowd cheers, and Santa presses his palm against the tree. A surge of power emanates from the Heart, and he visibly glows for a minute. When the wave hits me, I feel invincible for a time, at least until it fades when Santa steps back.

He bows to the crowd. "I have to continue the journey." With a wave, he returns to his sleigh. "Merry Christmas to all." With a flick of the reins, the reindeer run a short distance before jumping into the air and taking flight. That same red and green vortex briefly appears as they depart through it, then seals behind them as a phantom, "And to all a good night," echoes around us.

I stare, still shocked but warmed by the experience, while the rest of the townspeople start to party. As the celebration kicks into full swing, Frost takes my hand, leading me away from the crowd. We find a quiet spot near the Heart of Haven, which now pulses with vibrant, healthy energy.

"I'm so glad you came here," he says softly. "Everything has changed, at least for me."

I look up into his eyes, which are currently dark blue with silver sparkles, seeing the depth of emotion there. "I... I don't even know how to process everything that's happened. A week ago, I was just an accountant from Chicago. Now I'm apparently a fae with magical powers, standing in a hidden town full of magical creatures, holding hands with the most incredible man I've ever met."

Frost chuckles, pulling me closer. "I am, aren't I?" He winks. "Life has a way of surprising us, doesn't it?"

As snowflakes begin to fall gently around us, he tilts up my chin. Our lips meet in a kiss that sends sparks of magic coursing through my body. It's tender and passionate, filled with promise and the excitement of new beginnings.

We rejoin the celebration, hand in hand, as I contemplate the twists and turns my life has taken. Who knew that a simple visit to a small town would lead to discovering my true heritage, unlocking magical powers, and finding love?

This Christmas in Evershift Haven has changed everything.

Chapter 8

THE TOWN SQUARE BUZZES with activity as we rejoin the festivities. Colorful banners and twinkling lights dance through the air, settling into place as if nothing unusual had happened. I stand in the middle of it all, my mind reeling from the events of the past few hours.

Suzette and Throk approach. He has his arm around her, and she's snuggled close. She grins at me. "Look at you, all magical and everything." The teasing fades a bit. "How are you handling it?"

"I'm still processing it all," I say. "Last week, I was crunching numbers. Today, I'm channeling fae magic and helping save magical towns."

Frost chuckles. "You've taken to it remarkably well."

"I suppose I have," I say, surprised by my own calm. "It's like...I've finally found a piece of myself I didn't know was missing."

Suzette nods. "You've been looking for the right thing for a long time." As Throk takes her hand to pull her into an intricate dance, she waves at me before being swept away.

When it's just the two of us again, Frost's expression turns serious. "As you know, I've seen your face in my dreams for many years. I've been waiting for you."

I nod. "It sounds crazy, but I believe you."

He nods. "Thank you, but there's more." He pauses, looking pensive. "I think I'm in love with you."

The world seems to stop. I stare at him, open-mouthed, but no words come out.

"I know it sounds crazy. We've only just met technically, but I've known you in my dreams for so long, and today, working with you, seeing your courage and your innate connection to magic... Everything we went through confirmed everything I feel."

I take a step back, overwhelmed. "I don't know what to say."

He reaches for my hand, and I let him take it. His touch sends a spark of heat through me. "I'm not asking you to feel the same way yet," he says softly. "I just wanted you to know, and I don't want to rush you for an answer, but I hope you'll stay in Evershift Haven to explore this connection between us, to learn more about your magic, and be open to the future I've foreseen."

I look around the square, at the impossible beauty of this hidden world. Then I look back at Frost, and the hope shining in his eyes. "What about my life back home? My job, my apartment, my family..."

"We can figure all that out. The town has ways of smoothing over absences in the human world, and your family can visit. I know in my heart you belong here. You must feel it too."

I do feel the magic thrumming through my veins, and the sense of rightness I've experienced since arriving here, but it's all so sudden, so overwhelming. I'm risking a lot just imagining the idea of staying. "I need to think."

Frost nods. "Of course. Take all the time you need."

I walk away, my mind a jumble of thoughts and emotions. I end up at the edge of The Whispering Woods, the leaves rustling with secrets, and recall their earlier teasing, relayed through Candice and Throk.

"What should I do?" I ask the trees, not really expecting an answer.

To my surprise, a gentle voice whispers back. "Follow your heart, child of two worlds."

I laugh, shaking my head. Now I can hear them? I guess the extra magic I absorbed during the healing spell for the Heart of Haven made the difference.

I think about my life back in the "real" world. My tidy apartment, my predictable job, and my routine. It was comfortable, but was it fulfilling? Here in Evershift Haven, in just a day, I've experienced more wonder and excitement than in years of my old life.

And then there's Frost. The connection between us is undeniable. The way my magic responds to his, and the electricity I feel when we touch. It's too soon to call it love, but it's definitely something worth exploring. Just thinking about making love with him again is almost enough to persuade me to stay, and that's before I factor in emotions.

I make my way back to the town square, where he anxiously awaits. He looks tentatively hopeful when I reappear, giving me a small smile.

"I've made my decision." I give him a big smile.

Frost's smile grows. "And?"

"I want to stay. I want to learn about my magic, about this world, and..." I look into his eyes, currently a warm brown, like pools of melting chocolate. "I want to see where this thing between us goes."

His face becomes radiant in his joy. He pulls me into a hug, lifting me off my feet and spinning me around. When he sets me down, we're both laughing. "You won't regret this. I'll show you wonders beyond your wildest dreams."

"I'm counting on it," I say, grinning. "Not every day has to be a big adventure though. Just being here with you, getting to know you better, is more exciting than anything waiting for me in the human world."

He leans in, and this time, I meet him halfway. Our lips touch, and it's like a fireworks display behind my eyelids. I feel our magic intertwining, creating something new and beautiful.

When we break apart, we're both breathless. "Wow," I whisper.

Frost grins. "That was..."

"Magical?" I suggest, laughing.

He joins in my laughter. "Exactly."

The party continues, and Grizelda looks better and better. After about twenty minutes, her complexion brightens as the pallor of magical lethargy fades from her green skin. Her wild purple hair seems to regain some of its usual vibrancy, swirling gently around her face as if caught in an unseen breeze. The symbiotic magic exchange between Santa and Evershift Haven has clearly worked wonders.

She and Atlas are quietly arguing about her need to rest. She's insisting she won't need an entire week, and he's adamant. When she seems to continue resisting, he picks her up and puts her back in the bed still in the town square. I can't help laughing, which catches her attention.

Grizelda's eyes twinkle mischievously as she turns to me. "Hello, Evony. It seems we have quite the fae prodigy in our midst."

I feel my cheeks warm. "I'm still not sure I believe all this."

"Oh, trust me, darling. That magic you wielded? Pure fae energy." Grizelda winks. "You should stick around. Frost could use someone to balance out that icy personality of his."

Frost raises an eyebrow. "I resent that implication."

I glance between them, uncertain. "I... I am staying. At least for a while."

Grizelda claps her hands together, her eyes lighting up. "Wonderful. We must get you settled properly. How about I whip up a little house for you? Something cozy... Perhaps a charming daffodil cottage?"

I blink, trying to picture living inside an oversized flower. At least it would smell better than an onion. "That's very kind, but—"

"You aren't building houses or doing anything else for at least a week, love," says Atlas firmly. His voice sounds like two rocks rubbing together.

"She can stay with me," Frost interjects smoothly a beat after Atlas. "I have plenty of room in my poinsettia house."

My eyes widen. "Your what now?"

His lips curl into a smile. "My home. It's made from a poinsettia. A gift from Grizelda years ago. Would you like to see it?"

Curiosity gets the better of me. "I... Yes, actually. I would."

Grizelda waggles her eyebrows suggestively. "Ooh, moving in together already? My, how things progress quickly around here." She titters. "Like the town evokes love and magic." She winks at me.

My cheeks are hot. "I..."

"Don't tease," says Frost, his cool hand finding mine. The touch sends a shiver of magic up my arm. "Evony is still figuring out everything."

Grizelda's knowing smile widens. "Of course. Don't let me keep you lovebirds. Go on, enjoy the rest of the celebration. Oh, Evony?" Her expression softens. "Welcome to Evershift Haven. Truly. I'm always available to build a house if—"

"After next week," says Atlas.

The witch gives him an exasperated look and rolls her eyes, but she doesn't argue.

I imagine he's going to have his hands full trying to keep her from overdoing it again. I nod as a lump forms in my throat. "Thank you."

Frost gently tugs my hand, leading me away from Grizelda and back into the heart of the festivities. The town square is alive with music and laughter. Fairies dart between floating lanterns, their wings leaving trails of sparkling dust. A group of elves harmonize near the Heart of Haven, their voices weaving a spell of joy and contentment over the crowd.

"This is incredible," I whisper, taking it all in.

He squeezes my hand. "It gets better every year. Though I must say, this is the most exciting Yuletide I've experienced in centuries."

I turn to him, curiosity piqued. "How old are you exactly?"

He grins, a mischievous glint in his eye. "Old enough to know better, but young enough not to care. Let's just say, I've seen my fair share of Christmases."

We weave through the crowd, stopping occasionally to sample magical treats or admire enchanted decorations. I try a mug of "Reindeer Radiance" hot chocolate that makes my nose glow red for several minutes. Bella tells me it's a tweak on her previous recipe. It tastes more like raspberry than mint as an undertone, and I nod my approval.

By the time the glow fades, Frost introduces me to a group of ice sprites, who create intricate frost patterns on my skin with a touch of their fingers.

As the night wears on, I start getting tired. The adrenaline of the day's adventures is finally wearing off, leaving me pleasantly exhausted.

Frost notices my fatigue. "Ready to call it a night?"

I nod, stifling a yawn. "I think so. It's been quite a day."

He smiles softly. "That it has. Let's slip away. I'll show you to my home."

I should protest, since I have a room at the "Moonlit Inn," but I'm dying to see his poinsettia house—and be alone again with him. We make our way to the edge of the square, bidding goodnight to those we pass. As we leave the bustle of the celebration behind, a hush falls over us. The streets of Evershift Haven are quieter now, lit by softly glowing lanterns that float alongside the path.

"It's not far," he says, leading me down a winding lane. "Just behind the ice shop." The houses we pass are a whimsical assortment of shapes and sizes. I see dwellings that resemble everything from acorns to miniature castles.

We round a corner, and I gasp. Before us stands a house unlike any I've ever seen. It's shaped like an enormous poinsettia, its vibrant red petals forming walls and roof. The windows glow with warm light, and a wreath of holly adorns the door.

"Welcome to my home," he says, a hint of pride in his voice.

"It's beautiful," I say, taking in every detail.

He leads me up the path, waving his hand to open the door. As we step inside, I'm enveloped in warmth and the scent of cinnamon and pine, with the faintest hint of a floral note, probably from the poinsettia. The interior is cozy yet spacious, with high ceilings that mimic the curve of poinsettia petals.

Furniture of polished wood and soft fabrics in shades of green and gold fill the space. The walls are petals but hard, like Candice's onion house.

"This is amazing," I say after dropping my hand from the nearest wall to turn in a slow circle to take it all in.

"Let me give you the grand tour," he says, leading me through the living room. "This is where I spend most of my free time."

A massive fireplace dominates one wall, its mantle adorned with intricate ice sculptures that don't seem to melt. Bookshelves line another wall, filled with tomes both ancient and modern.

"The kitchen," he says, gesturing to an open space, where copper pots hang from the ceiling, and a large island stands in the center. "I'm not much of a cook, but the appliances are enchanted to follow recipes perfectly."

We move upstairs, where Frost shows me a guest room and his study. Finally, we reach the master bedroom. It's a large, circular space that forms the center of the poinsettia. The domed ceiling is enchanted to show the night sky, stars twinkling above us.

"And this is my room," he says softly, looking at me.

The air between us suddenly feels charged with electricity. I take a step closer to him, drawn by an irresistible force. "It's beautiful," I whisper.

Frost's hand comes up to cup my cheek. "Not as beautiful as you."

Our lips meet, and it's like fireworks exploding behind my eyelids. I feel our magic intertwining, creating something new and beautiful. Frost's arms wrap around me, pulling me closer, and I melt into his embrace.

"We should slow down," I whisper against Frost's lips, but my fingers are already working at his shirt buttons.

"Should we?" His voice is husky as he walks me backward toward the bed, scattering kisses along my neck. My sweater drops to the floor, followed by his shirt. Each step leaves a new piece of clothing behind like breadcrumbs.

When my fingers trace his chest, his skin is deliciously cool, making me gasp. "You're so cold."

"And you're burning up." He traces my collarbone, leaving a path of sparks that makes me shiver. "So beautiful," he murmurs, mapping my body as if for the first time. His touch is delicate, purposeful—featherlight caresses that leave trails of tingling magic skittering across my skin.

When we come together, stars explode behind my eyes. Our magic weaves together, gold and silver strands braiding in the air around us, amplifying every caress, every sensation. I open my eyes to see the enchanted ceiling transforming—ribbons of green and purple aurora dance overhead, shooting stars streak past, matching the rhythm of our movements.

"Look," whispers Frost against my ear, and I watch as constellations rearrange themselves, creating patterns I've never seen before. The magic builds between us like electricity, like starlight, or like the first snow of winter meeting the last warm day of fall.

The stars above us shift and dance, creating new patterns I've never seen in any astronomy book. My magic mingles with Frost's, creating swirls of gold and silver light that spiral upward toward the enchanted ceiling. The sensation is indescribable—like diving into a pool of starlight.

"The constellations." I gasp when his cock swells as he pumps deeply into me while still watching as they form intricate designs. "They're beautiful."

He traces a path down my neck with his lips, each kiss leaving a trail of cool fire. "They're responding to our magic." He slides his hands down my sides, leaving trails of sparks in their wake. "Watch."

As he sinks into my pussy again, I lift my hips to meet him. When we move together, the stars above pulse in rhythm. Gold and silver strands of magic weave through the air around us, creating a cocoon of light. The temperature in the room fluctuates—my heat meeting his coolness in perfect balance.

"I never knew it could be like this," I whisper, arching into him as pleasure builds. Even the time in the bubble wasn't this intense. It was before my magic fully awakened. The aurora overhead intensifies as ribbons of green and purple dance across the ceiling.

He threads his fingers through my curls, which are surprisingly warm now despite his natural coolness. "Neither did I. Our magics are perfectly matched."

Each touch sends new sparks of power through me. The stars overhead spin faster, creating spirals of light that mirror our movements. My skin tingles everywhere we connect, magic flowing between us like electricity as we thrust against each other, straining for fulfillment.

"Open your eyes," he murmurs against my lips. "Look at what we're creating."

I do and gasp at the sight. The entire room glows with our combined magic. Frost's silver light twines with my golden power, creating patterns that pulse with each shared breath. Above us, the constellations have formed into shapes I recognize from ancient texts—the eternal lovers, the twin flames, and the sacred union.

He slides his hand down my back, leaving trails of frost that my inner fire instantly melts. Steam rises where our skin meets, adding to the otherworldly atmosphere. The magic builds higher and stronger until it's hard to tell where his power ends and mine begins.

"You're incredible," he says against my neck, grazing my skin with his teeth and sending new shivers of pleasure through me. "So responsive to magic."

I run my fingers through his silver hair, watching as golden sparks follow my touch. "It's you," I say. "You make me feel..." Words fail as another wave of sensation washes over me.

The aurora overhead brightens, casting multicolored light across our skin. Where the light touches, our magic responds, creating swirls of power that dance across our bodies. The temperature continues to fluctuate—hot and cold, fire and ice, perfectly balanced.

Frost captures my lips again, and I taste winter—crisp and clean like fresh snow. His tongue slides against mine as our magic surges higher. The stars above spin faster, creating a vortex of light that mirrors the building pleasure.

"Look," he whispers again, breaking the kiss to direct my attention upward. The constellations are moving more rapidly now, forming new patterns with each passing second. "They're showing us our future."

I watch, transfixed, as the stars form images—two figures intertwined, surrounded by swirling magic. The vision shifts, showing scenes I can barely comprehend before they change again. Through it all, our bodies move together, magic building between us like a gathering storm.

The room fills with our combined power, golden light mixing with silver until it's impossible to tell them apart. Each touch brings new sensations—frost melting against fire, winter meeting summer in perfect harmony. The pleasure builds higher, stronger, until I think I might shatter from the intensity. When we come simultaneously, the light show flares like the Big Bang, so bright I have to close my eyelids and look away even as pleasure consumes me.

Afterward, we lie tangled together, our breathing slowly returning to normal. Frost traces patterns on my skin, leaving little trails of frost that quickly melt away.

"I never... That was..." I trail off, unable to find words adequate to describe the experience.

Frost chuckles softly. "Magic?"

I laugh, snuggling closer to him. "That'll do, but somehow, it's still not a strong enough descriptor."

He nods before we lie in comfortable silence for a while, basking in the afterglow. The events of the past few days swirl through my mind—discovering magic, saving Evershift Haven, and now, this connection with Frost. It's all so overwhelming, yet it feels right.

"Frost?" I say softly.

"Hmm?"

I prop myself up on one elbow. "I can see myself being very happy here."

His expression brightens with joy. "Really?"

I nod, a smile spreading across my face. "Really. This place, this magic, you... It all feels like home somehow. Like I've found a part of myself I never knew was missing."

Frost pulls me closer, pressing a kiss to my forehead. "I'm so glad to hear that. I've waited centuries for you."

"Centuries," I say, tracing the line of his jaw. "I still can't wrap my head around how old you are."

He grins mischievously. "Age is just a number when you're magical, as you'll discover. I expect you'll stop aging now that your magic has awakened, and you're in Evershift Haven. Don't worry about being with an older man though—I promise, I've got the energy of someone much younger." He winks.

I laugh, swatting his chest playfully. "I don't doubt that for a second."

We fall into comfortable silence once more, the enchanted ceiling above us now showing a peaceful forest scene. Moonlight filters through the leaves, casting dappled shadows across the bed.

"So," I say after a while, "What happens now?"

Frost props himself up, looking down at me with a mixture of excitement and tenderness. "Now, we start your magical education in earnest. There's so much for you to learn, and so many wonders to explore, and I'll be right here beside you every step of the way."

The prospect sends a thrill through me. "I can't wait."

Frost's eyes twinkle with mischief. "First, how about another lesson in fae magic and consummation energy?"

I grin, pulling him down for another kiss. "I thought you'd never ask."

MUCH LATER, I NESTLE deeper into Frost's embrace. The events of the day swirl through my mind—discovering my magic, saving Evershift Haven, and now this incredible connection with Frost. My eyelids grow heavy, and I drift off to sleep, lulled by the steady rhythm of his breathing.

In my dream, I'm in a sun-dappled meadow. Wildflowers of every color imaginable sway in a gentle breeze, their petals shimmering with an otherworldly iridescence. The air is filled with the tinkling laughter of children.

Two small figures dash through the tall grass, their giggles echoing across the field. As they draw closer, my breath catches in my throat. They're twins—a boy and a girl, no more than five years old. The boy has Frost's silver-white hair and my warm brown eyes, while the girl sports my dark curls and Frost's changing eye color. Their skin tone is light brown, and a perfect blend of both of us.

"Mama? Papa?" they call out in unison, racing toward us.

I glance to my left and see Frost standing beside me with joy. He kneels down, arms outstretched to catch the children as they launch themselves at us.

"There are my little snowflakes," he says, scooping them up and spinning them around. The twins shriek with delight, their laughter like music.

I reach out to touch the girl's cheek, marveling at the perfect blend of Frost and me in her features. "What are your names, little ones?"

The boy puffs out his chest proudly and answers for her. "I'm Jasper, and this is my sister, Aurora."

Aurora nods enthusiastically. "We're learning magic, Mama. Watch this."

She holds out her tiny hand, scrunching her face in concentration. A small flame appears in her palm, dancing and flickering. Jasper, not to be outdone, creates a miniature snowstorm in his hand.

"Fire and ice," murmurs Frost, his gaze meeting mine over the children's heads. "A perfect balance."

I laugh, feeling a surge of pride and love. "Just like us."

The scene shifts, and we're suddenly in a cozy living room. A Christmas tree towers in the corner, its branches laden with enchanted ornaments that twinkle and move. Jasper and Aurora sit cross-legged on the floor, eagerly tearing into presents.

"Look, Papa," says Jasper, holding up a tiny broom. "My first flying broom."

Frost chuckles. "No flying in the house. Your mother would have my head if you knocked over her favorite vase again."

I swat his arm playfully. "As if you didn't encourage them last time."

Aurora squeals with delight as she unwraps a crystal ball. "It's just like Auntie Grizelda's."

"And just as dangerous in the wrong hands," I say, raising an eyebrow at Frost. "I hope you've childproofed that thing."

He winks at me. "Of course, love. It only shows the future of their toy collection for now."

The dream shifts again, and we're back in the meadow. The twins are older now, maybe ten or eleven. They're practicing more advanced magic, their faces set in identical expressions of concentration.

Jasper waves his hand, and a sapling sprouts from the ground, growing rapidly into a young tree. Aurora touches its trunk, and the leaves burst into vibrant autumn colors.

"They're getting so strong," I murmur to Frost, leaning into his side.

He nods, pride evident in his voice. "They take after their mother."

I snort. "Oh, please, Mr. I've-been-practicing-magic-for-centuries. They get plenty from you too."

As if to prove my point, Jasper creates an intricate ice sculpture with a flick of his wrist—a skill he definitely inherited from Frost.

The scene changes one last time. We're in the Evershift Haven town square, decorated for some kind of celebration. Banners proclaim, "Congratulations, Graduates!" Jasper and Aurora, now young adults, stand before us in ceremonial robes alongside other children around their age. I see both Suzette and Candice among the crowd of proud parents.

Grizelda, her wild purple hair streaked with more silver now, beams at the twins and other young adults around her. "By the power vested in me as the guardian of Evershift Haven, I hereby declare you full-fledged members of our magical community."

The crowd erupts in cheers. Tears prick my eyes as I applaud, overwhelmed with pride and a touch of nostalgia. When did they grow up so fast?

Frost squeezes my hand. "They'll do great things," he whispers.

I nod, unable to speak past the lump in my throat. Our children—a perfect blend of human and fae, of fire and ice, of logic and magic. They represent everything I never knew I wanted, everything I never believed could exist, and everything I now can't imagine living without.

As the dream begins to fade, I hear Frost's voice, distant but clear. "Evony? Love, wake up. You're smiling in your sleep."

I blink awake, the vivid images of the dream still fresh in my mind. Frost is propped up on one elbow, watching me with a mixture of curiosity and affection.

"Good dream?" he asks, brushing a stray curl from my forehead.

I nod, still caught between the dream world and reality. "The best," I whisper, snuggling closer to him. "I saw our future, Frost. Our children."

His eyes widen. "Jasper and Aurora."

I nod, not surprised he knows their names. "Twins. A boy and a girl. They were beautiful, and so magical." I recount my dream to Frost. With each detail I share, his eyes grow brighter, and his smile wider. By the time I finish, we're both a little misty-eyed.

"It sounds perfect," he says, his voice thick with emotion.

I caress his cheek. "It does, doesn't it? But it was just a dream. We have no way of knowing if—"

He silences me with a gentle kiss. "Fae dreams have a way of coming true. Especially when they're born from love and magic in a place like Evershift Haven."

I gaze into his eyes, seeing the future I dreamed reflected there. "I hope you're right," I whisper.

Frost grins, a mischievous glint in his eye. "There's only one way to be sure. Shall we start practicing?"

I laugh, pulling him down for another kiss. As our bodies entwine, and our magic mingles, I can almost hear the echoes of children's laughter in the distance. A promise of the future, waiting to unfold.

About Aurelia

AURELIA SKYE IS THE pen name *USA Today* bestselling author Kit Tunstall uses when writing science fiction and paranormal romance, along with paranormal women's fiction. It's simply a way to separate the myriad types of stories she writes so readers know what to expect with each "author."

If you enjoyed this story and would like to receive notifications of new releases or access bonus chapters for your favorite books, please join my Mailing List[1]. You'll also receive free books just for joining. If you prefer to receive notifications for just one, or a few, of my pen names, you'll have the option to select which lists to subscribe to at signup.

---

1. http://kittunstall.com/newsletter/

Also by Aurelia Skye

Alien Baby Pact
Baby For The Brundle Commander
Baby For The Serp General
Alien Baby Pact Compilation
Baby For The Grimlock General
Baby For The Palantir Chief
Baby For The Alphan Captain
Baby For The Mosaic Med Chief
Baby For The Tark Commander

Alien Baby Pakt
Alien Baby Pakt Zusammenstellung

BioCircuit Nexus
Cyborgs' Origins
Cyborg's Tether
Cyborg's Love

Celestial Mates
Wrong Place, Right Mate
Destined For The Drakari Warlords

Guerriers Blessés
Chassé
Inlassable
Marqué
Justice
Compilation Guerriers Blessés

Harrow Bay
Hell Gates & Hot Flashes
Nightmares & Night Sweats
Warlocks & Wrinkles
Love Spells & Liver Spots
Phantasms & Presbyopia
Vampires & Varicose Veins
Mermaids & Mood Swings
Séances & Sagging Skin
Necromancy & Knee Pains
Marids & Memory Loss
Devil Deals & Dizzy Spells
Happy Endings & New Beginnings
Harrow Bay, Volume 1
Hellhounds & Mistletoe
Harrow Bay, Volume 2
Harrow Bay, Volume 3
Harrow Bay Complete Series

Harrow Bucht Serie
Höllentore & Hitzewallungen
Alpträume Und Nachtschweiß
Hexenmeister & Falten

Liebeszauber Und Leberflecken
Phantasmen Und Alterssichtigkeit
Vampire und Krampfadern
Meerjungfrauen Und Stimmungsschwankungen
Séancen Und Schlaffe Haut
Nekromantie Und Knieschmerzen
Marids und Gedächtnisverlust
Teufelsgeschäfte Und Schwindelzauber
Happy Ends Und Neuanfängen
Höllenhunde & Mistelzweige

Hell Virus
Catching Hell
Surviving Hell
Bleeding Hell
Raising Hell
Sharing Hell

Howls Romance
The Jaguar Alpha's Forbidden Lover
CEO Wolf Shifter's Surprise Twins

Northstar Shifters
Northstar Heir's Scarred Mate

Olympus Station
Station Commander's Surrogate
Alien Prince's Secret Baby
Security Agent's Alien Bartender

Olympus Station Compilation

SpicyShorts
Music In My Heart
Kilted Tentacle Monster: A Search for True Love

Sweet Escapes
Hook & Wendy

The Haunting of Clara Gray
Ghostly Awakening
Ghostly Harmonies

Three Crones Inn
Vastly Inn-proved
Ghastly Intentions
Grave Inn-tervention
Ghostly Inn-heritance
Three Crones Inn Compilation

True North
True North #1: Death & Deception
True North #2: Rescued & Revelations
True North #3: Fire & Ice
True North #4: Enemies & Lovers
True North #5: Truth & Tiranog
True North #6: Fight & Flight

True North #7: Love & Loss

Wounded Warriors
Relentless
Marked
Justice
Wounded Warriors Collection
Hunted

Standalone
Reluctant Companion
Princess By Mistake
Fire Lord's Assistant
True North
Dragon Laird's Witch
Alien General's Rebel Consort
Tempted By Demons
Enemy Combatant
Grotesquerie
Mistaken Bounty
Wahre Richtung
Power Surges & Amorous Urges
Taken By The Orc General
Compilation Alien Baby Pact

Also by Kit Tunstall

After The End
Unraveling
Unyielding

Cybernetic Hearts
Cœurs Cybernétiques: Série Complète

Evershift Haven
Howls & Harvest
Winter Wishes & Elven Kisses

Howls Romance
CEO Wolf Shifter's Surprise Twins

TnT Storybuilders
Building Your World: A Guide For Writers
Action Thriller Storybuilder: A Guide For Writers
Instant Love Novelette Storybuilder
Instant Love Novella Storybuilder: A Guide For Writers

Contemporary Reverse Harem Novel Storybuilder
Contemporary Romance Novel Storybuilder
Cozy Mystery Novel Storybuilder
Dark Romance Storybuilder
Gothic Romance Storybuilder
Ménage Novelette Storybuilder
Ménage Novella Storybuilder
Ménage Novel Storybuilder
Paranormal Revere Harem Storybuilder
Paranormal Romance Novel Storybuilder
Psychological Thriller Storybuilder
Regency Romance Storybuilder
Science Fiction Romance Novella Storybuilder
Spicy Novella Storybuilder
Sweet Novella Storybuilder
Romantic Suspense Storybuilder: A Guide For Writers
Postapocalyptic Thriller Trilogy Storybuilder
Horror Novel Storybuilder

Standalone
Holiday Tales: Four Short Stories of Thanksgiving and Christmas
Master's Gift
Dragon Laird's Witch
Baby Daddies: Older Men & Babies Collection
Christmas Kiss: Limited Edition Six-Story Holiday Collection
Sampler: SF, Contemporary & Historical Collection

Watch for more at www.kittunstall.com.